25

D0091073

A
Harlequin
Romance

OTHER
Harlequin Romances
by MARY MOORE

MATAI VALLEY MAGIC

by

MARY MOORE

HARLEQUIN BOOKS   TORONTO
WINNIPEG

Original hard cover edition published in 1973
by Mills & Boon Limited

© Mary Moore 1973

ſ

SBN 373-01712-X

Harlequin edition published August, 1973

Printed in Canada

CHAPTER ONE

FERN FRASER opened her eyes, then shut them again quickly; the bright light made her head ache abominably. She knew she was in hospital, and that she had been moved into a larger room, and . . . and . . . She went to sleep again.

The next time she woke up a nurse was standing beside her. 'Feeling better?' and a thermometer was poked into her mouth and that saved her having to answer. The nurse's hand felt cool on her wrist.

'Would you like a drink? There's a fruit drink on the locker beside you. Do you think you can manage?'

Fern tried but could not reach it, so the nurse handed her the glass and steadied her while she took several sips.

'Nurse, could you please tell me how I got here, and what's wrong with me?'

'You were in a car accident and the ambulance brought you in. Don't you remember? The crash, I mean?'

Fern tried to concentrate, but to no avail. 'Sorry, I can't even remember being in a car.'

The nurse smiled pleasantly. 'Don't worry, that's quite normal. You've been unconscious for twenty-four hours, and have some concussion. Your memory may come back and then again you may never catch up on the missing bits. Either way, it's not important. You only need a bit of rest and you'll be as good as new. You were very lucky really, just a bump on the head, and a few stitches in your foot. Did you see the gorgeous flowers that came for you this morning?'

Fern turned her head slowly, feeling a sudden movement might make it fall off. She gasped as she saw the magnificent basket of flowers. 'Who sent them?'

'Mr. Alexander. He was driving the car, and has been very worried about you. He wasn't hurt, but they kept him in hospital overnight for observation. He's going home this afternoon, but I'm sure he'll be in to see you before he leaves. He's over seventy, and has had quite a shake-up, but all he's done is drive us mad with questions about your progress. I gather you were hitch-hiking and he picked you up, then shortly afterwards the accident occurred. Any more questions?'

'No. I just feel tired, I think I'll go back to sleep.'

'Good idea. Next time you wake up you'll feel much better.'

Fern had another look at the flowers. Mr. What's-his-name must be a nice old man to be so concerned. She drifted off to sleep again. Some time later she became aware of men's voices close to her bed. She wanted to see who it was, but her eyelids felt so heavy she just lay there half awake, half asleep, listening.

'Well, are you satisfied now? She looks all right to me.'

'Poor little thing! The nurse did say she was just sleeping, didn't she? How can they tell if she's asleep or unconscious ... You can see she's lost a lot of blood, she's so pale. She was as bright as a button, a real cheerful little girl, chattering away nineteen to the dozen while we were driving along. I feel wretched about the whole business.'

'So you should. I've warned you about picking up hitch-hikers. It's a very bad policy. You're fortunate that she's still alive, the way you drive. Now, let's get home. You've seen that she's okay.'

That was a young angry voice, Fern decided. The other voice must belong to the old man who had been driving the car. There he was again. 'Don't be in such a hurry, Brett. I'd like to wait for her to wake up. Just to tell her I'm sorry. And she isn't okay. You were with me when the doctor said that they put thirty stitches in her foot and had to give her a blood transfusion the night they brought her in. And what about her concussion? The doctor said it might give her trouble off and on for years. He said any damage to the brain had to be treated as serious.'

The strong, impatient voice broke in, 'He also said she

6

would probably have no permanent damage, just a few headaches for a while. You needn't bother waiting to tell her you're sorry ... my guess is that you're going to have plenty of time for that. These footloose and fancy free types that get around the country bludging rides instead of paying their way usually have a pretty good knowledge of the law. You'll probably find yourself in court with a whopping damages claim.'

'She wasn't a girl like that. I told you, she was a nice wee thing.'

'Huh! Want a bet? When she finds out you've got a bit of money she'll hire a smart lawyer and take you to the cleaners properly. And serve you right, you silly old sentimental goat. Nice wee thing! You ...'

'You shut up!'

Both men jumped. Fern was awake with a vengeance. Her huge angry brown eyes seemed too big for her small white face. 'You've got no right to bully an old man, nor to take away my character before you've even had a chance to speak with me. I have no intention of putting in a claim against your father. He gave me a ride, and I'm grateful, even if I can't remember anything about it. I've never been to a lawyer in my life. So just because you've got a mercenary streak in your make-up don't judge everyone by your own standards!' Then to Fern's consternation she burst into tears.

The old man was very upset. 'There, there, dear. Here, use my handkerchief. Don't take any notice of that stupid oaf. And don't you worry, I'm going to look after you. The doctor said they'd like to keep you in hospital a few more days, and then you can come and stay at my farm provided I take you into town each day to get your foot dressed. You'd like that, wouldn't you? You told me you were having a good look round, and weren't tied to a timetable.'

The old man looked so genuinely anxious that Fern managed to stop crying. 'Sorry about that. I'm not usually the weepy sort.' She gave a wavering smile. 'It's very kind of

7

you to invite me to your home, but I'll manage just fine when I get out of here. You must be the person who sent me the lovely flowers. Thank you very much. They're absolutely splendiferous.' Her smile was much more successful this time.

'Alexander, that's my name, Hamish Alexander. I'm glad I thought of the flowers.' He took Fern's hand. 'Promise me you'll come and stay at Matai Valley when they let you out. I know you've got nowhere else to stay. You told me that when we were in the car.'

Fern felt too exhausted to argue. 'If you really want me to, but I don't think your son will approve.'

'He's not my son. If I had a son he'd have better manners than this young jackanapes. He's my nephew, and if he doesn't approve of you coming to me it will make your visit all the more enjoyable. Promise, now.'

'Yes, I will. Thank you.' She twisted a little to see how the young man with the angry blue eyes and dark hair was taking it. He looked very disapproving, but obviously was not going to dispute his uncle's invitation.

Mr. Alexander stood up. 'We'll be off now, and let you get back to sleep. The hospital will let me know when to collect you. Is there anything else you need? Can I get in touch with your people . . . you know, tell them you've been in a crash and that you're all right, and that I'm looking after you? It would relieve their minds.'

Fern shook her head, and was immediately sorry as she winced with pain. 'Not to worry. They wouldn't be interested in the slightest.'

Mr. Alexander snorted, 'Fine sort of parents you've got, young lady, if they don't care whether you're dead or alive.'

That wasn't what Fern meant and she was just going to correct the false impression when the tall, tanned young man, Brett, gave a short laugh. 'You sure know all the right cards to play to get the right tune on Uncle's soft heart!' He walked out of the room.

8

Mr. Alexander peered at her. 'You won't let him make you change your mind?'

'Never,' Fern answered with fervour. What an arrogant, ill-mannered young man!

'Good. I see you and I are going to get along fine, my dear. Good-bye now, and get well quickly. You and I are going to have some fun together.'

He patted her hand several times, then said good-bye and left. Fern liked him. He was small and thin and had a brown weather-beaten face and bright blue, mischievous eyes, and a neat, well-trimmed goatee beard.

Yes, they would have fun together. She drifted back to sleep.

Next morning in the mail Fern received a parcel. She unwrapped it quickly and found two shortie nightgowns, each one a dream of shirred nylon and lace. One was a fuchsia shade and the other sea-spray. Although there was no note with them she knew Mr. Alexander to be the donor. He must have noticed the hospital gown of butcher's blue stripes which she had been wearing yesterday. A tall, blonde staff nurse admired them. 'Almost worth getting run over to get these! Which one do you want first . . . this bluey green would be my choice. Come on, I'll help you change. They tell me you had a hilarious time in the shower this morning . . . Nurse Bronson was so particular about keeping your bandage dry that she ended up getting most of the water.'

Fern felt miles better in the dainty feminine wear, and found the strength to do her long dark hair. It was a slow, tedious job because the nurses had been afraid of hurting her, and so had lightly smoothed it with their hands. One of the walking patients had gone down to the shop to buy her a brush and comb and some talc.

The following day an enormous carton of fruit arrived. It was so artistically arranged it seemed a shame to eat any, but Fern couldn't resist the huge strawberries, and lifted one punnet from the box before asking the nurse to put the

9

carton on the windowsill for the other three patients in her room to help themselves, and the staff also, whenever they came in during the day. They were at first reluctant, but as Fern pointed out quite logically, she could not eat them all if she stayed a month, and then they happily obliged.

When the doctors came on their rounds the next day, they examined Fern's foot, pronounced that it was healing nicely and again mentioned how fortunate she had been that no tendons were cut. When Fern managed to wriggle around and get her first look at the angry hook-shaped gash on the instep of her foot she agreed wholeheartedly. After a few searching questions they told her she could be discharged that day, providing she could attend a doctor each day to have her foot dressed.

The Sister-in-Charge, who had been accompanying the doctors' round, slipped over and said, 'I'll let Mr. Alexander know you're ready to leave. He's been ringing regularly for news of you, so I should expect him to call shortly after lunch. As soon as your foot has been dressed you can get up and put your clothes on.'

Fern lay quietly. Clothes. She really had not thought about her pack since the accident. She would have to make inquiries. It might be in the hospital somewhere.

When the staff nurse had replaced the dressing and bandaged her foot, Fern asked about the pack.

Staff Nurse Roberts replied, 'As far as I know you only have what you were wearing at the time of the accident. I'll check the personal effects list.' She opened the top drawer of the locker. 'Hm. Bra, briefs, jeans and top, scarf, wristwatch, and wallet containing ten dollars and forty-five cents, driver's licence, personal papers, and – oh, one sandal. No pack, perhaps the police took charge of it, or the old man. After all, it was probably left in the car.'

'I suppose my clothes will be a mess?'

Staff Nurse laughed, 'Well, I've got to admit they were a bit bloody when you came in, but one of the girls laundered them for you.' She took them from the locker. 'Can you manage by yourself?'

'Sure can. And please thank whoever washed my gear. I really do appreciate that kindness. In fact, I've been so well looked after that I feel a bit sad to be leaving. Honestly, the view from these windows is just fabulous. The sea changes mood every hour, and I've never seen such spectacular sunsets. You'd think each night as the sun lowers down and sinks into the Tasman Sea that someone was running a competition to see which night could produce the most vivid colours, the most varied cloud layers. It must help people to regain their health much more quickly . . . and the staff. I've noticed as you each come into the room you look out across the Sea for a moment. You must find it relaxing when you're rushed off your feet, or feeling tense and anxious with a difficult or particularly ill patient.'

'You could be right. I've never noticed it. Perhaps it's an automatic reaction by now. Now I must leave you. Mr. Alexander said he'd be here about two o'clock this afternoon. Oh, you said something about feeling sad at leaving. People who have been concussed, even slightly, often get a little depressed at times until they're fully recovered. I thought I'd mention it. If you know what to expect it won't worry you too much. If it feels worse than an odd fit of the blues then do mention it to the local doctor.'

Fern managed to put on her underwear and faded striped T-shirt without much effort, but it was a different story trying to get her heavily bandaged foot through her jeans, even though they flared from the knee. By the time she slid to the floor to zip up her jeans and cinch the wide leather belt around her slim waist, she was perspiring and shaking. She sat down in the comfortable lounge chair with a sigh of thankfulness.

Mrs. Marshall, the lady in the next bed, smiled and said sympathetically, 'You're not feeling too grand, by the look of you. It's always the same when you first get up and dress. You'll have to take it fairly easy for a while.'

Mrs. White from across the room, who had also been

given permission to go home, came over. 'My, those pants don't owe you anything! But you're looking better, your colour is coming back now.'

Fern patted her faded threadbare jeans defensively, although she knew the remark was quite without malice. Well, she had no choice. If she had known she was going to end up in hospital she just might have worn something different.

'Can I help you pack up, dear?' Mrs. Sinclair offered.

Fern grinned, 'I've not got much, only two nightgowns and a hairbrush, etc., and nothing to pack them into.'

Afer lunch, Fern felt much better and attempted one or two short walks around the room. He foot was bandaged so firmly in the crêpe bandage that it felt quite comfortable, except once when she overbalanced and put all her weight on it. She felt the perspiration break out on her forehead and had to steady herself on the windowsill for a few seconds before she could move again.

At two o'clock she was sitting by her bed, clutching a brown paper bag containing her belongings, a happy, expectant look on her small, bright face. She was eagerly awaiting Mr. Alexander's arrival so that she could thank him for her presents. When his nephew came striding into the room and towered over her, her smile froze.

'Where's Mr. Alexander? They said he was coming to get me.'

'My name is Alexander too. If you want Uncle Hamish, you'll have to wait until you get home. He's not well, and has to stay in bed. If you're not happy to see me, I can assure you that the feeling is mutual.'

Fern grimaced, 'Charming! What pretty manners you have.' Nevertheless, she stood up carefully. 'I'm ready when you are.' She really had no choice.

'You can't walk out of here barefooted. Where are your shoes?'

Fern glared at him, then opened the paper bag, pulled out one very worn sandal and thrust it towards him. 'I have only one, the other must have been torn off in the accident. I can't wear this one because it makes me put too much weight on my sore foot.'

'Do you mean to say you have only one pair of shoes?'

'Why not? I can only wear one pair at a time.'

Fern walked from the room and started slowly down the corridor towards the lift, stopping every few yards to say good-bye to the nurses who had taken care of her. One of them offered her a wheelchair, but she refused, laughing, 'I'll make it, given time.'

Brett moved closer. 'Why didn't you accept? It will take ages getting out of this place at this rate.'

'You go ahead if you don't like to be seen with me,' Fern replied angrily.

'As a matter of fact, I was thinking it would be easier on you. However, now you come to mention it, you are a pretty scruffy-looking kid. Of course, I realize that it's the in-thing for your sort to dress in rags and be allergic to soap and water, as if there was some virtue in being dirty. Which group do you belong to, the beatniks? hippies? . . . or just a plain drop-out?'

Fern stopped. 'Take your pick. But one thing you can be sure of, I'm quite clean. I had a shower this morning, and washed my hair, so you're not likely to catch any bugs from me.' She swung round, her brown eyes flashing. 'You talk of "my sort" in derogatory tones, but your sort smell of money, and that's not a special virtue in my eyes, so stop looking down your well-bred nose at me. Do you think you're superior just because you've got a pair of shoes on and . . .'

Fern gritted her teeth against the wave of pain that swept over her and clung to the rail that ran along the corridor.

The next minute she was swept off her feet, and Brett strode grimly towards the stairs, ignoring her protests to be put down.

Then, with Fern still held firmly in his arms, he went rapidly downstairs, out through the main doors of the hospital, and round to the car park.

Fern was completely helpless in his iron grasp and to her

further humiliation felt the tears running down her cheeks. Oh, she could kill him!

Changing his grip suddenly he opened the door of a Holden Utility and pushed her inside. 'Fasten your safety belt.' He shut the door and walked quickly around to the driver's seat.

Fern brushed the tears away angrily and obediently clipped the diagonal strap over her shoulder.

Brett drove over the bridge and turned sharply to the right, heading south.

'I suppose you feel almighty pleased with yourself, picking me up like a bag of flour and carrying me out of the hospital in such an undignified manner. Well, it doesn't impress me. Brute strength may appeal to some, but not to me.'

'I wasn't trying to impress you, young lady, if I may be forgiven the title as applied to you. You acted like a brat, so I treated you as I would treat any child having a tantrum.'

Fern sniffed rudely, and decided to ignore him. It was a beautiful drive from Greymouth to Hokitika, with the road running parallel to the sea, and on the left the glorious sweep of the Southern Alps.

As they drove into Hokitika Brett asked, 'Is there anything you want before we leave town?'

'Yes, I want to buy a pair of sandals, please,' Fern replied coldly.

Brett swung the car into an angle parking area right infront of a shoe store.

'That suit you?' Brett looked at her a bit diffidently. 'Do you need help to get in there?'

'No, thank you,' was the icy response.

As Fern opened the door he spoke again. 'Do you have any money?'

Fern held on to the door, and pulled her wallet from her hip pocket, extracted her ten-dollar note and offered it demurely. 'Sure, do you want a loan?'

'Oh, get on with it. I haven't got all day.'

14

Fern limped into the store and, taking her own sweet time, she chose a pair of strap sandals so that she could open the right one quite wide and fit it on over the bandage.

Back in the van she strapped herself in before inquiring pleasantly, 'I do hope I haven't kept you waiting too long?' knowing full well that he was fuming impatiently.

He reversed back into the street, and this time drove inland towards the mountains. Fern suddenly realized that she had no idea where the farm was situated – not that it mattered. All she hoped was that Brett Alexander lived a long, long way from Matai Valley.

Brett asked suddenly, 'Why wouldn't your parents worry if you had an accident? Are they the casual modern-type parents who've opted out of responsibility for the kids?'

'Surprising as it may seem to you, my parents are eminently respectable. Real squares, if you prefer it that way.'

'Poor bods! What a disappointment you must be to them.'

Fern gurgled, 'Don't be too sorry for them, they're bearing up magnificently. Of course having three other children in the family helps. You would approve of my sister and my brothers, all working away busily at their careers.'

'Then why don't they stop you drifting around?'

'How? By chaining me to the bedpost?'

'But you're so young. Surely they could have done something,' he persisted. 'It's not safe for a child of your age to be hitch-hiking around on your own.'

Fern smiled, 'How old do you think I am?'

'About seventeen or eighteen,' he guessed.

Fern's smile widened. At twenty-four, she was well used to being taken for a teenager, and usually was very indignant, but today she thought it was a hilarious joke. As Brett was so sure of himself, it delighted her to see him jump from one wrong conclusion to the next.

He darted a glance at her, then said severely, 'I see by that happy smirk on your face that you're probably even younger than I thought. Well, get one thing straight, you're not going to make a fool out of my uncle. He's a bit . . . shall we say eccentric. He has a heart condition and mustn't become over-excited or worried. I'm very fond of him, and I promise you that if you hurt him in any way, I'll make you very, very sorry. He seems to have taken quite a fancy to you, and rather than upset him I've let him have his way, but remember, I'll be watching you. One false move and out you go.'

Fern's smile disappeared . . . smirk indeed! she thought angrily . . . and warning her not to hurt Mr. Alexander . . . as if she would!

'There's no use looking sulky. I live with him, and when I'm not there Kirsty will be, and you'd better not start any nonsense with her around. She'll soon sort you out.'

'Sounds like a game of Happy Families.' Fern was utterly dismayed. This exceedingly stuffy young man actually lived in the house! No wonder Mr. Alexander needed a bit of light relief in his life. Fern would see he got it if it was the last thing she did.

CHAPTER TWO

As they turned at the crossroad which had an attractive tavern as a centrepiece Brett spoke again. 'We'll soon be home. I hope you've been giving some thought to what I said.'

Fern, who had simply been enjoying the drive and admiring the well-cared-for farms along the rich fertile valley, the large herds of sleek dairy cows and the modern farmhouses, said quite honestly, 'No.'

They crossed a long narrow concrete bridge spanning the Kokatahi River and drove some distance before Brett swung into a driveway lined with macrocarpa trees, and swept round in a circle to park in front of a large comfortable house.

He came quickly round the ute and opened her door. 'You needn't think you can put me off with that "little girl lost" look – I'll bet you're as hard as nails. If I hear of you wheedling money or presents out of Uncle Hamish I'll see you leave even faster than I brought you here.'

Fern ignored him until she was standing upright on the cement path. She felt stiff and sore even though the utility's seat had been comfortable. The long drive had served to remind her that she had several large bruises on her hips and back as well as her cut foot to contend with.

'Sorry, I didn't realize that your main concern was that your uncle might spend money on me. Well, you can forget it. I came here because your uncle invited me, and because the doctor said I must. I'll leave as soon as I can walk. Now get your notebook out and I'll give you a list of all the things I've taken from Mr. Alexander. One basket of flowers, one box of fruit which I shared with the other patients at the hospital, and two nightdresses.' Fern angrily pulled them out of the brown paper bag and flung them at him.

It gave her the utmost satisfaction to see him fumbling with the froth of lace and nylon, a look of shocked embarrassment on his face. She limped to the open door of the kitchen and walked in.

'You'll be Miss Fern Fraser?' A tall, elderly woman was standing by the window, and as she turned, Fern guessed by the barely concealed laughter in her grey eyes that she must have witnessed the whole incident. 'I do think you'd better keep those pretty nighties, somehow I don't think they would look half so well on Brett.' She walked forward and shook Fern's hand. 'You're very welcome, my dear. My name is Kirsty. Now, come along through to the lounge; Mr. Alexander is there and very impatient to meet you.'

Fern followed Kirsty into the next room, admiring the elder woman's erect posture and stately bearing. So this was Kirsty, who would be also keeping an eye on her. Somehow the prospect didn't daunt her much; even though Kirsty had a stern face and wore her grey hair pulled back severely in a bun, there had been that gleam of humour in her eye. Fern felt that given time, she would be able to get along very nicely with Kirsty.

'Ah, there you are, Fern. Brett took a devil of a time collecting you, I must say. Kirsty, do we get a cup of tea? Come here, girl, sit down and tell me how you feel.'

Kirsty stood in front of them. 'You well know, Mr. Alexander, that the kettle's on the boil. You'll have your tea and scones as always, and after that Miss Fraser will be going to her room for a rest until dinner-time. Anyone with half an eye can see she's exhausted and in considerable pain.'

When Kirsty left the room Mr. Alexander pulled a face. 'I'm supposed to be the boss here, and I get ordered around by that woman, not to mention Brett always interfering. A man can't call his soul his own. But you and I are going to get on famously. I'm relying on you to help me escape their restrictions. They work hand-in-glove with old Doc Walters. He was out here last night, pretending he was worried about my heart, when everyone knows he just came out

18

for an evening's fishing. Says I've got to rest for a week, just so he can have first go at the fish!'

'What's wrong with your heart?' Fern asked.

'Not a damned thing. They just use it for an excuse to keep me under.'

Fern chuckled, 'They don't seem to be doing a very good job.' She went on to thank him for his gifts.

Kirsty came in with the tea tray and placed it on the occasional table. 'Milk, Miss Fraser?'

'Please call me Fern, and yes, I do like milk in my tea. Can I do anything to help?'

Kirsty glanced up. 'No, you sit where you are and keep Mr. Hamish quiet and happy, and you'll be doing us all a favour.'

The old man winked at Fern as she settled back on the carpet beside his chair. She eased her new sandals off, and felt much more comfortable.

'Ah, here you are, Brett,' Kirsty said, handing him a cup of tea. 'Scone?'

'Thanks, Kirsty. I won't sit down. I'll just have mine and run. 'I'm late now.'

'You'll sit down, Brett. It takes just as long to drink a cup of tea either way.'

Fern accepted her cup from Kirsty and bent forward so that her long dark hair swung forward, hiding the smile on her face, as Brett sat down ... apparently she wasn't the only one Kirsty could sort out!

Mr. Alexander asked, 'Did Brett take good care of you on the way home, Fern? I'm sorry I couldn't go for you myself.'

'I'm sorry, too, Mr. Alexander, but Brett ... well, Brett behaved exactly as I would have expected.' She smiled up at him, her brown eyes beguilingly innocent.

'Good, good.' The old man was satisfied. He leaned foward and stroked Fern's hair. 'What do you think of my find, Kirsty? I like the way young girls wear their hair long just as they did when I was a young fellow.'

19

Kirsty was quiet for a moment, then: 'Yes, I think long hair is most attractive. A woman's crowning glory.'

Brett stood up and put his cup on the tray. 'And do you find bare feet also attractive, Kirsty, not to mention girls wearing men's pants?'

'I don't find them any more objectionable than a young man being rude to a guest of the house,' said Kirsty sharply, 'I'm sure Fern will change into something more suitable for dinner. Now come with me, young lady, I have your bed nicely warmed and I'm sure you need a rest.'

As Fern followed meekly behind Kirsty, she flicked a glance at Brett and then smiled directly at him for the first time. To Fern it was perfectly obvious that neither of them had won that round. Kirsty had clobbered both of them. Brett did not smile.

The first thing Fern's eyes alighted on when she reached her bedroom was her pack. 'Oh, I am glad, I thought I might have lost it.' She unbuckled it happily, while Kirsty turned down the bed.

'Have you a dress there which you would like me to iron?'

Fern replied, 'No, thank you. Most of my things are in non-crushable material.'

When Kirsty left the room, Fern stood looking out the window for a few minutes. The bush-clad hills beyond the river were purple in the afternoon sun, and still further back were the snow-covered mountains. Even though it was early summer the sun had not yet succeeded in melting the last heavy snows of the late spring. She turned back to the bed and was surprised at how tired she felt.

It seemed only a few moments later that a knock on her door woke her, and Brett said loudly, 'Kirsty says it's time you dressed for dinner. I hope you get the emphasis on the word "dress".'

Fern sat up, rubbing her eyes, then muttered, 'Drop dead!'

'I'm glad you heard me.'

She heard Brett's footsteps receding and thought grumpily that they could probably hear him in Australia. She felt much better after washing her face and hands, and then had difficulty in deciding what to wear. If she had thought she could annoy Brett by wearing her jeans she would have had no hesitation in wearing them; but then again she did not want to upset Kirsty. Finally she decided on culottes in brown and green.

She wound her long hair into a soft chignon, applied eyeshadow with a subtle hand, and then outlined her mouth with a frosted lipstick. She stood away from the full length mirror trying to assess the effect.

Yes, the soft, filmy material of the culottes swung and floated with her every move, the long batwing sleeves and the high mandarin collar and line of tiny covered buttons from neck to waist made it extremely feminine gear.

Brett and Mr. Alexander stood as she entered the room and Kirsty paused in her work and eyed her up and down. 'Now, that *is* neat and tidy.'

Mr. Alexander gallantly offered her his arm to escort her to the table. 'You'll never become conceited while Kirsty is around. Neat and tidy, my foot. You look as glamorous and elegant as any film star.' Then his wicked mischievous eyes swung to Brett. 'Aren't you going to compliment our charming guest on her attractive appearance?'

Brett replied, 'I'm quite sure she has no need of my approval.'

Fern's brown eyes challenged him across the table. 'That's extremely fortunate, because I'm sure it would be a long time coming.'

Brett's blue eyes narrowed. 'I must say you seem reasonably intelligent,' he said scathingly.

Fern giggled, and deliberately misunderstanding him, said gaily, 'Oh, you *do* know how to flatter me. I would much prefer to appeal to you because I'm clever rather than because I'm beautiful.'

Kirsty joined them at the table and Fern saw Brett visibly

force himself to refrain from the biting retort which leapt to his lips. He wasn't laying himself open to Kirsty's reprimand again.

Mr. Alexander laughed, giving every evidence of enjoying the thrust and parry between them.

Throughout the meal the conversation was mainly between Mr. Alexander and Fern, although Kirsty joined in from time to time. Her remarks were short, and direct, and were given with a certain dry humour which Fern found delightful.

As they moved away from the table after the meal Mr. Alexander remarked, 'Your mother showed remarkable sagacity when she named you Fern when you were a tiny baby.'

'Why do you say that?' Fern asked, with a smile.

'Well, I'm not usually given to a poetic turn of phrase, but I have no difficulty in seeing you, especially in that long greeny-brown gown, as someone who would blend into the forest ... your long dark hair and big brown eyes; your slender young neck ... you have the same fragile look of the fern, yet they also have surprising strength and hardiness, as I suspect you have. What do you think, Kirsty?'

'If you mean she's as thin as a rail, I'll agree – all this dieting and modern food fad nonsense.'

Brett laughed, 'I agree with you, Uncle, she wouldn't be out of place in the bush. You find all sorts of strange things there – stinging nettles, bush lawyers, vines, not to mention deadly nightshade.'

Kirsty ignored Brett. 'Fern, if you would take Mr. Hamish into the lounge and settle him?'

Mr. Alexander bristled. 'I'm not a baby, woman, and if you don't stop treating me as such, I'll be giving you your notice!'

'And if you don't follow the doctor's orders I'll be taking it,' Kirsty said crisply. Fern gathered that both threats were empty ones. She followed Mr. Alexander into the lounge, gave him the evening paper, then his glasses, and switched on the television set for the news.

'Is there anything else before I go and help with the dishes?'

'Yes, put another stick on the fire. I like a black pine fire. Although it's October, there's still a bite in the evening air.'

Fern put a small log on the fire and checked the fire-screen. 'There's a bite in the air all right, and its name is Brett.'

The old man chuckled happily. 'Yes, you do seem to annoy him. That's good, just what he needs. He's far too serious these days.'

As Fern returned to the kitchen she heard Brett: '...Yes, it's a damned nuisance, Kirsty, but I suppose I'll have to take her in. It's going to be a bit of a drag taking time off each day to get her to the doctor.'

Fern interrupted, 'You don't have to take me in. Isn't there a bus service?'

'No.' Brett wasn't the least bit put out that she had over-heard his remarks.

'Well, I have my driver's licence. I'm a reasonably competent driver. Why can't I drive myself into Hokitika?'

'Competent by whose standard? If you think I'll let you have my new Holden you can think again. As you've helped Uncle wreck the Viva, there's only the farm ute left, and we can't afford to be without that. If you wrap it round a tele-phone post, what then? You be ready at ten-thirty tomorrow morning.'

He picked up his jacket. 'I'd better get moving if I'm to get to the meeting on time. Sorry I can't give you a hand with the dishes, Kirsty.'

'I can help Kirsty,' Fern said indignantly.

Brett stood in the doorway. 'You can't, you know. We've often tried to get Kirsty to get help in the house, but she says she'd leave if she has to put up with another woman in the kitchen. So you get back in to Uncle and entertain him. That's what you're here for. Good night, Kirsty.' He went

23

out, closing the door behind him.

Fern just stood there staring at the door. She felt sick. Brett had shown her what a nuisance she was coming here ... and if she wasn't even allowed to help Kirsty without upsetting the whole household! She bit her bottom lip, feeling the treacherous tears stinging her eyes.

'There's a clean pinny on the end of the table. No need to soil your pretty clothes.'

It was a moment before the implication of Kirsty's words sank in. 'But Brett said ...'

'Brett is responsible for the farms, and no light task it is. But in the kitchen ...' Kirsty left the sentence unfinished, but there was no doubting her meaning.

Happily, Fern tied the large apron around her slim waist, and picked up the tea-towel. 'Hasn't he any help on the farm, Kirsty?'

'Indeed, yes, he has. Ross Smith and his wife, they live in the house through the trees. See the lights? That's the new house. It was built for Brett's father when he married.' She sighed and was silent for a considerable time. 'Then there's young Robbie, a farm cadet, but I'm thinking it would be wrong to say he's a help on the place.'

Fern's heart went out to young Robbie; they'd be two of a kind. 'Why couldn't one of them drive me into town, if it causes Brett such inconvenience?'

'That's for Brett to decide.' Kirsty's tone brooked no further discussion on that subject.

Fern slept late next morning and woke to find Kirsty by her bed with a breakfast tray.

'Oh, I'm sorry. I didn't mean to have you carrying meals to me. You should have called me.'

Kirsty waited for her to sit up. 'Fiddlesticks! It's no trouble. You see you eat it all up. You must stay in bed till ten, then you can have a bath, and be ready to go with Brett. You've had a very nasty accident, and it's God's blessing that you're not worse hurt. Have you slept well?'

'Yes, I had a wonderful sleep. This is a lovely room. You must find this big house a lot of work.'

'I manage. I suppose it's just routine for me now, I've been here close on twenty years. My man and I had a small farm down where the rivers join. My cousin Grace came to visit us just before the war and she married Donald Alexander, Brett's father. The war came and Donald and my husband went away to war together. Donald came home and when Brett was born – ah, what plans they made! They bought the next door farm and built the new house. My man didn't come home, but I hung on to the farm. We'd worked so hard to get it, and Donald and Hamish gave me a hand when they could. Then Grace and Donald were killed in a car crash when Brett was about six. Hamish came to me and asked me to come and keep house for him and help him bring up the boy. So I did. In a way I was glad to sell him the farm, it was such a struggle for a woman to keep it going.' She looked at Fern and saw the warm sympathy in her brown eyes. 'Here's me blethering away here and your breakfast going cold. I must away to my work.'

'Thank you for telling me, and thank you for my breakfast.' But Kirsty was gone.

Fern was very thoughtful as she ate her more than generous breakfast. She wondered how much heartbreak those few short sentences had covered. Kirsty and her young husband striving to get a farm of their own, and then his going off to war and not returning. Then the struggle for her to keep the farm; and giving in, when her cousin Grace and her husband were killed, to come here and bring up their child.

But what puzzled Fern most was the question, why *had* Kirsty told her? Her instinct told her that Kirsty was not a great talker, and certainly not someone who would normally share family confidences at the drop of a hat.

Finally she gave up the problem and went through to the bathroom. It was more difficult trying to have a bath without the help of Nurse Bronson, but eventually she managed and dressed once more in her faded flares and tan skivvy. She parted her hair in the middle and caught it above each ear in leather thongs. She gazed in the mirror with dissatisfaction; no wonder Brett took her for seventeen or eighteen. She caught her hair and held it behind her head; would she look older if she had it cut short? She shrugged her slim shoulders. Who cared what Brett Alexander thought?

She put her pack in the wardrobe and made her bed, and went out to the kitchen.

'Good morning, everyone. Is there anything I can do to help?'

'Yes, Fern, put out the cups and saucers, I've just brewed the tea. Then get some shortbread out of the blue tin in the pantry while I butter this date loaf.'

Fern's eyes danced wickedly as she saw the astonishment on Brett's face. So Kirsty wouldn't let anyone help her in the kitchen, wouldn't she? A fat lot he knew!

'You're looking a lot better this morning, Fern,' Mr. Alexander pronounced. 'A few days of this good country air, and you'll be as fit as a fiddle. You tell Doctor Walters that he needn't think he's going to have me confined to barracks much longer. As soon as you can get about, I'm going to show you the farm. Can you ride?'

'I've been on a horse once or twice, although I doubt if you would call it riding. But if you've got some quiet old horse I'd love to have a go.'

'Right, Brett, you get one for her. And while you're in town call at the garage and see how long they'll be getting my car back on the road.'

Brett looked at him. 'Does it matter how long it takes? You're not allowed to drive any more. The doctor said he should have put his foot down long ago. If he'd done so you wouldn't have had this last smash.'

'Och, old Walters doesn't know what he's talking about. I'm as good a driver as I ever was.'

Brett grinned, 'And that's not saying much! You're a proper menace on the road. If it wasn't that everyone knows

26

you, and makes allowances for the fact that you never use road signals, you'd have come to grief long ago. And I mean it – you're not allowed to drive again.'

'Who said anything about me driving? Young Fern here will take me around, won't you, my dear?'

'I'd love to, Mr. Alexander,' Fern said with relish, especially happy to be doing something to help the old man, and at the same time annoy Brett.

Brett stood up. 'Are you ready for town?'

'I'll just get my bag.'

Fern went to the passage door and heard Brett call after her, 'And your shoes.'

She came back in a few minutes with her shoulder bag on, and carrying her sandals. Brett was already in the car, and she joined him.

As he drove off, he asked, 'Is it against your principles to wear shoes?'

'No.'

'I guess that was a silly question. Your sort don't have principles, do they? They think the world owes them a living, that rules were made to be broken. I suppose you're one of those placard-waving clots we see trotting around the city, in protest marches. Pity you couldn't find a job and do a decent day's work.'

'You know, that's an idea.' Fern hesitated, then grinned, 'A bad one, but still an idea.'

'What's wrong with working for a living?'

'Nothing, if you like it. But why should I work? I've got everything I want. You know the old song "I've got the sun in the morning and the moon at night". Well, everyone can have that whether they work or not.'

'You mean you're quite content to get around the country, cadging rides, living on anyone who's silly enough to ask you in?'

'Whatever you say.'

'You're a parasite, living off the people who do work,' he said savagely. 'I'm disgusted.'

27

Fern laughed happily. 'And I bet it makes you feel like a million dollars.'

'Why do you say that?'

'Because it's true. There's nothing so ego-building for your sort as making snide remarks about people who have different values from yours.'

She saw him stiffen. The rest of the journey was made in angry silence. He parked the Holden in front of a big two-storied house.

'Is this the doctor's surgery?'

'Yes, just go along the drive, and you'll see a notice on the door. This is our family doctor. If you prefer it I'll take you down to the centre of town to a younger doctor. In fact you can have the choice of two others if you so wish. Actually it's a bit of a favour for Doc Walters to see you. He doesn't take new patients: he's semi-retired.'

'He'll suit me fine,' Fern answered. 'Are you going to wait?'

'I've got Hobson's choice, I guess.'

Fern walked along the drive feeling the cement warm under her feet. She saw a notice, 'Ring and Enter' and followed the instructions.

The waiting room was empty, and she had barely time to sit down when the surgery door opened.

'Come along in.' Doctor Walters was a big man, tall, broad-shouldered with a shock of snow-white hair. 'You're the young lady who led old Alexander astray?'

'Fern Fraser.'

'Yes, Miss Fraser, take a seat and tell me what's worrying you.'

'The hospital doctor said I should get this dressed each day.' She lifted her foot.

'Right, first things first. Hop up on the couch.' He took the bandage off. 'Hmm, you were lucky. Seems to be healing nicely.' He dressed the wound, then bandaged the foot carefully. 'Feeling okay?'

'Yes, thank you.'

'Well, what's next? Your head giving you any bother?'

'No, not really, a sort of dull headache occasionally, nothing to worry about.'

He looked at her keenly. 'Well, what *are* you worrying about? Come on, spit it out. No use pussy-footing around with me.'

Fern sighed. 'If I tell you something about myself, will you treat it as confidential, or will you feel you have to tell the Alexanders?'

Doctor Walters sat regarding her seriously for a few seconds. 'Will it hurt them or worry them not to know what I'm to be told?'

Fern answered honestly, 'No. In fact I think it would upset them if they did know.'

'I'll take your word for that, but I'll reserve my decision until I've heard what you've got to say.'

After taking a deep breath, Fern started, 'Well, it's like this. They think I'm a hippie or drop-out or whatever. It gives Mr. Alexander a great deal of pleasure to think he's dropped a cat amongst the pigeons, so to speak. I think he'd be dreadfully disappointed if he found out I was sailing under false colours. He's a darling, but enjoys teasing Kirsty and Brett.'

'And how do they react?'

'Kirsty surprisingly well, except that I have to change out of this gear for dinner. I thought at first she saw me as a brand ripe for plucking from the fire, but on second thoughts I think I've misjudged her.'

'And Brett?'

'Total disgust. I'm a parasite, a bludger, a cadger, and I'm sure he'll come up with some others given time.'

Doctor Walters smiled, 'And his bad opinion of you doesn't trouble you?'

'Not a bit.'

'Why are you confessing to me? I mean, if it is a confession.'

Fern swung her feet down over the couch, fished into her

bag and pulled out a certificate. Still holding it, she explained, 'Having to bring me in here each day is an imposition on Brett, and he has let me know how inconvenient it is.' She handed the certificate to the doctor. 'You see, I'm a registered nurse. I could do this dressing myself, if you'll let me.'

'Hmm! Trained in Wellington. If I agree don't you think they'll smell a rat?'

Fern gave him an appealing smile. 'Not at all. I'll say I worked in a hospital once and picked up a bit of knowledge. They think I've been bumming around the countryside, so haven't a clue where I've worked.'

'I'll go along with you, if you promise to come in immediately if you see any change for the worse in that wound, although it seems a good clean cut.'

'Thanks a million.' Fern's small, heart-shaped face was bright with relief. She prepared to slide down to the floor.

'Hold it!' Doc Walters barked. 'I'm not letting you get away with half a story. Why are you wandering around the country aimlessly?'

Fern settled back on the couch while she watched helplessly as the doctor sat down, and leisurely filled his pipe and lit it.

Then she said tentatively, 'Brett is in a hurry, and I don't like to keep him waiting.'

'Are you on holiday?'

'No . . . well, yes.'

'That's what I like, clear decisive answers.' The doctor puffed away on his pipe. 'Had a quarrel with your boyfriend?'

'Not really.'

'There is a boy somewhere, then?'

'There was a few months ago. Not now. Can I go now?' Fern pleaded.

'Nope. Fair's fair. You asked me a favour, now I want to know why. And don't worry about Brett, he can wait. After all, you're going to save him driving in here every day for the next week.'

Fern came to the conclusion that she wasn't going to get out of this surgery until she had given this exasperatingly persistent old man the full story. 'I'm twenty-four.'

'You don't look it . . . but carry on.'

'Oh, it sounds so silly. Won't you leave it until another time?'

'The longer you dither, the longer you'll be here,' Doctor Walters remarked relentlessly.

After several false starts Fern finally got going. 'I was watching T.V. with my mother and father one night . . . oh, several months ago. It was about two young people travelling around the world, they even had a baby with them, and they seemed so happy and carefree even though they didn't know where they'd sleep the next night or if they would eat . . . you know sort of "take no care for the morrow" kind of thing, and I suddenly got fed up with my life, in fact I felt I was getting older, and life was passing me by. So I said to my parents, that's what I wanted to do . . .'

Doc Walters prodded, 'And how did they take it?'

'Oh, they were marvellous. They just said "Get going".' Fern stopped, then went on with a rush, 'That's half the trouble. Other kids, friends of mine, went through hell when they were teenagers, fighting with their parents – you know, the generation gap, and all that junk . . . while my parents are super. I've never had to struggle for anything, not even for understanding. Then I seem to have spent my life in institutions, every move regulated. Five years at boarding school, the four training at the hospital – I was suddenly fed up to the back teeth. Half the girls in my class at school were married with a couple of kids . . . the same with my nursing class . . . either married when they were training or when they finished, and the others gone abroad. I kept getting letters from them, from London, Canada, or Timbuctoo. And my life was dull, dull, dull!'

'Have you any brothers or sisters?'

Fern sighed. 'Yes, I guess that just added to the whole

thing. Duncan and Tony, my brothers, and Rata, my sister . . . well, they're brilliant. I'm not kidding, they really are. They call me "Mouse" – I guess I was behind the door when they handed out the brains and good looks, or else someone reckoned our family had its quota already. I'm the one that got "reliable, responsible, a good pupil" on my reports. Oh, I told you this would sound crazy.'

'No, I'm really interested. Carry on.'

Fern laughed, 'Well, you've got the worst of it. My father said to give my notice in at the hospital, take ten dollars and only what I could carry in my pack, and take off for a year. When I left, they said they didn't want to hear from me, unless it was an emergency. I was to work when I wanted and needed to . . . I mean if I wanted to eat.'

'And how has it worked out?'

'It's been fun. I spent last autumn in Nelson picking apples, then went on the tobacco work. I've been a waitress – oh, all sorts of jobs, but it really hasn't changed me. I'm still me. That's what makes it so funny to have the Alexanders take me for a hippie. I guess I just haven't got the right mentality . . . I don't smoke grass, I don't sleep around, I work till I've got a bit ahead, instead of trusting to luck . . . so you see my father was right. He said go and find yourself, and I have. I'm conservative, mediocre and downright dull.'

The doctor's bushy eyebrows raised. 'I wouldn't agree. But tell me something, did you envy your family their brains or good looks? Did you envy your friends their married status?'

Fern slid to the floor. 'No. That's what makes it so stupid. I could have been married by now if I wanted to. I had a steady boy-friend, but honestly, by the time I went with him for over a year, it was just like going out with one of my brothers. I liked him, but marriage? Heck, no! As for brains, I'm not thick . . . I've got enough to get me through exams, not with honours, mind you, but a pass, which is all I wanted, and I don't envy Rata her beauty, she always seems to be getting into scrapes. Can I go now?'

Doctor Walters got to his feet. 'Yes, grilling session over. Here, I'll give you these dressings for your foot. I'll see you Friday to take out the stitches. I'll walk out to the car with you.'

As they walked out the path Fern asked, 'Could I take the stitches out myself?'

'I think that the Alexanders would find that hard to credit. In fact, I think you're going to find it difficult to keep the rebel act up, if you stay too long.'

Fern giggled, 'I'm fairly right there ... my brothers belong to an anarchist group at Varsity, so I've just got to swap sides and use the arguments that they used to use on me.'

The doctor was still laughing when he arrived at the car. 'Hello, Brett, how's life?'

Brett watched Fern get in. 'Not so bad, Doc. We have a few problems, but I think I can handle them. Uncle Hamish is pulling on the chain a bit. I don't know how long we'll be able to keep him inactive. Well, I suppose I'll see you tomorrow?'

'No, not till Friday. This young lady has a bit of first-aid knowledge. She'll do her own dressing till then.'

Brett called at the garage and then headed for home. 'So you managed to con old Doc Walters as well?'

Fern laughed, 'I've always preferred older men. Men your age are too cynical.'

'You mean we're too wide awake to your tricks.'

'Could be,' Fern answered blandly.

CHAPTER THREE

NEXT morning Fern woke as the sun rose over the Big Mountain and streamed directly into her room. She dressed in her brown stretch trews and green skinny-rib top, and tied her hair back in a thick soft braid of green wool.

'Good morning, Kirsty. Isn't it a lovely day?' she said as she entered the kitchen, and reached for her apron. 'What can I do to help?'

'Good morning. You should have stayed in bed,' Kirsty replied, but after taking one look at Fern's fresh young face she relented. 'You do seem much improved. Set the table for breakfast, and a tray for Mr. Hamish.'

By the time she had taken Mr. Alexander's breakfast into him and stayed to chat a few minutes, she returned to the kitchen to find Brett seated at the table.

Apart from a brief, 'Good morning,' he ignored her, but talked away quite cheerfully to Kirsty. Obviously finding Fern at the breakfast table had not exactly made his day, but she had not ruined it entirely because he managed to enjoy his breakfast with a healthy appetite.

As Fern moved to help Kirsty clear the table, he asked, 'Have you dressed your foot this morning?'

Surprised, Fern replied, 'Not yet. I'll do it after I've done the dishes.'

'I'd like you to do it now. The dishes can wait.'

'Why should I do it when it suits you? It's my foot.' Fern continued clearing the table.

'You'll do it now so that I can see if you can dress it competently. If not, then I'll take you into town,' Brett explained patiently as if speaking to a retarded child.

Fern gave him a look of pure dislike, and went to her room to collect the new bandage and dressing. She put them on a chair near the colonial couch, then sat down and carefully unwound the bandage.

'Do you want me to boil the kettle for you?' Brett asked a little more pleasantly.

Fern did not look up from her task. 'No, thank you, *Doctor Alexander*, this type of wound requires a dry dressing.'

As she removed the previous dressing she noted that there had been a little bleeding, but no more than she had expected.

'May I see it?' Brett moved closer, then sat down at the end of the couch and took her foot in his hands. 'Look at that, Kirsty! She could have lost her foot.'

Kirsty, after a sharp intake of breath, said, 'Oh, you poor child! Can I help you in any way? That's a very awkward place to bandage.'

Fern smiled at her. 'It's all right. It looks much worse than it really is. And if Brett would give me back my foot, I'll get on with it. I wouldn't like Mr. Alexander to see it, he may get upset.'

Brett released her foot, but did not move away. He watched her clean the wound, powder it and apply the new sterile dressing, then skilfully and neatly put on the crêpe bandage.

She glanced at him, her brown eyes hostile. 'Satisfied?'

'Perfectly satisfied. Very professional,' Brett answered with exaggerated politeness. He stood up, looking down at her angry face. 'I hope that the accident has been a lesson to you. You could have been crippled or killed, but you have to expect things like that if you take rides with every Tom, Dick or Harry.'

'Oh, belt up! You're so smug and self-righteous! I don't suppose you've ever hitched a ride in your life. And why not? Because you've always had your own car. And I'm particular who I take rides from. For example, I would never accept a lift from you.'

'No danger. You wouldn't get asked.' Brett left the room, not quite slamming the door after him, but it was certainly shut very firmly.

Fern laughed at Kirsty, 'That sorted him out!'

Kirsty tried to stop smiling, but was unable to resist Fern's merry brown eyes. 'You should take heed of what Brett says. It isn't safe for a young girl to be getting around on her own. One poor lass was murdered down on the Haast Pass only a year or so ago. She was hitch-hiking.'

'Yes, I heard about that. I'll be careful not to ride in any murderer's car either.'

'Off with you! There's no use talking sense to a fool.' But the words lacked antagonism.

After Fern had put her things away in her room she washed her hands and joined Kirsty at the sink. They shared the mornings work amicably and when lunch time came Mr. Alexander complained bitterly that he hadn't invited Fern here just to become a household slave.

'I want to show Fern the farm. I want to show her the whole district, in fact. Did you find out how long they'll be with my car, Brett?'

'A fortnight or three weeks.'

'That's not good enough. If you're too niggardly to lend us yours, you can ring up and get me a rental one.'

'I didn't say you couldn't have my car. When do you want it?'

'Tomorrow.'

'Okay,' Brett said soothingly. 'I'll drive you wherever you want to go.'

The old man said furiously, 'I don't want you driving me, I want Fern. Then we can stop and I can tell her about places and people. You act as if an hour off the farm is an hour wasted. I'll not have you breathing down my neck!'

'Right, don't get upset. Fern can drive you if that's what you want.'

Mr. Alexander glared at Brett, reminding Fern of a small, indignant terrier attacking a dog three times its own size. 'I'm not upset. And I'm not begging for your blasted car. If I can't have it tomorrow and every afternoon Fern's here, you can get me a rental. I know what I want.'

Brett laughed, '*And* you always get your own way. I thought old age was supposed to mellow a person, but you get more mean-tempered every day.'

To Fern's amazement Mr. Alexander looked pleased, and was soon settling into a farm discussion with Brett. They became so engrossed that they did not notice Kirsty and Fern clear the table and wash the dishes. As Fern hung up the tea-towel, she said, 'Brett certainly knows how to handle his uncle.'

Kirsty nodded. 'And that's no easy job either. If you argue, he gets into a temper, but if he thinks you're soft-soaping him he gets worse.'

Mr. Alexander looked up. 'What are you two whispering about over there? Have you got Fern working again? I'll soon put a stop to that.' He got slowly to his feet. 'You come with me, girl. I'm going to show you round the farm buildings, and introduce you to Ross Smith and his wife.'

Kirsty gave Mr. Alexander his gumboots, and then handed a lighter pair to Fern. 'You'd better wear these if you're going to be traipsing over the countryside.'

Fern saw her watching Mr. Alexander anxiously, and saw the look of relief come into her eyes when Fern said, 'I'm not going too far. I don't want to hurt my foot.'

'No. No, we must be careful.' He took Fern's arm. 'We'll have a look-see at the cowshed first. As soon as Ross sees us heading that way, he'll be over to skite it off. We built it last year so that we could go on the tanker run, for the milk power factory. Ross is in charge of the dairy herd and Brett manages the sheep and cattle. Of course, they work in together a lot.'

'And Robbie?'

'He hinders them both.' As soon as they entered the shed two men appeared.

'Ha! Told you, Fern, didn't I? Ross is more proud of this shed than his own kids.'

'And why shouldn't I be? This shed helps me with my

work, a damn sight better than my kids ever did.'

'This is Fern Fraser. Fern, meet Ross Smith and Robbie Sinclair.'

Fern shook hands with them both. Ross Smith was a big, fair man with a pleasant smile. Robbie was of medium height, slightly built, with curly brown hair and hazel eyes. Fern liked them both. Ross showed them through the shed, of which Fern felt he had every right to be proud. It was of concrete and gleaming stainless steel, and was immaculately clean, reminding Fern of an operating theatre.

'You come back when we're milking, Fern, it'll be easier for you to understand everything if you see them working.' Ross Smith said.

'I'd love to,' Fern accepted with a smile. 'Can I come any time?'

'You certainly can, night or morning, and if you come often enough we'll have you in here working.'

Mr. Alexander growled, 'Oh, no, you don't. I found her. She's mine, and she's not here to work.'

Ross chuckled, 'Golly, I can't wait to get old! Fancy an old joker like you picking up a pretty young piece like this, and nobody raises an eyebrow. Now, if I turned up with Fern, my old woman would cut me into pieces with a blunt breadknife. Old age certainly has its compensations!'

After they left, Mr. Alexander conducted Fern on a grand tour of the woolshed, implement shed and sheep and cattle yards, finally walking back through the orchard and ending up at the new house.

Mrs. Smith gave them a warm welcome. 'Come on in. I've been dying to meet you ever since Robbie came home and said that Mr. Alexander had picked up a real smashing bird.' She led them into a bright comfortable room. 'And you're looking better, Mr. Alexander. This little bird must have been the tonic you needed.'

'Yes, she has brightened the old place up,' Mr. Alexander replied, as he sat down. 'Well, what's new about the district?'

38

'Take a chair, Fern. What's new, let me see? Pam Freeman has a baby girl. After getting three boys, I believe they've gone properly gaga about this wee one. It must be nice to get a girl – I never had such luck. I'd have loved a girl, they're such fun to dress up – not that I'd swop my two sons, of course.' She turned to Fern to explain, 'Both my boys are over in Australia working on some big project, making fabulous money. Now if I'd had a girl she might have married around here and we'd see something of her.'

Mrs. Smith was a small, plump woman with once dark hair now turning grey. When she smiled Fern saw a deep dimple in her remarkably unlined face. While Mrs. Smith talked on about the district affairs, Fern looked about her. This house was much more modern than the homestead. It had big floor-to-ceiling windows, which gave a wonderful view of the Alps. The furniture was modern too, and there were pot plants in every available space.

'Come through to the kitchen, Fern. We'll make a cuppa.' She passed Mr. Alexander a magazine. 'Ross was going to take that over to you, but now you're here you can read it while the kettle boils.'

Out in the kitchen she chatted to Fern. 'Sorry to hear about your accident. My, it's nice to have a young girl about the place. How's Kirsty taking your arrival? She can be a bit sticky sometimes.'

Fern smiled. 'She's been very good to me.'

'I'm glad of that. Well, remember, any time you want a chat drop in for a cuppa with me.'

'Thank you, Mrs. Smith, I'll remember that.'

'Call me Smithy! Everyone else does. Now you take the tea and sugar and I'll bring the rest. How long are you going to be with us?'

'About a week or ten days,' Fern replied as they returned to the lounge. 'I'll be leaving as soon as my foot is fit to carry me properly.'

'Why do you want to talk about leaving when you've just arrived?' Mr. Alexander said irritably, and he took his cup.

'You'll go when I say you can go.'

Next day Fern helped Kirsty with the work in the morning, and after lunch went out to where Brett had parked the Holden. Mr. Alexander was sitting waiting impatiently.

Brett opened the driver's door for her. 'I backed it out of the garage. We haven't got a drive-through garage and we don't want one, so see that you park it here when you get back.'

Fern got in and pulled the door shut. 'Not to worry. I've got every confidence in the driver.'

'Well, that makes one. You *did* say you could drive? That car is only a couple of months old. Show me your licence.'

Fern pulled it from her pocket and handed it to him. 'Sure you wouldn't like me to do a Road Code test for you?' She took the licence back angrily. 'Thanks for nothing!'

'It never hurts to check,' Brett remarked coldly.

Fern gave him a withering glance, then switched on the car and took off smoothly. Following Mr. Alexander's directions she turned left on to the main road. They crossed over the long Kokatahi River Bridge, but instead of turning towards Hokitika at the tavern they went straight ahead towards the hills. Mr. Alexander knew every inch of the road, every farm and family. They stopped frequently so that he could point out the attractive school set on the banks of a creek, the store and churches and hotel at Lower Kokatahi. Not only did he know who owned the farms now, but who had owned them forty or fifty years ago, and he captured Fern's full attention as he told anecdotes of families long left the Valley, not to mention the dramatic expansion in the district since the war.

He tapped Fern's arm. 'Stop here. Look over in that paddock.' Following his pointing finger Fern saw several deer – a large stag, two does, a yearling and a tiny fawn. 'Oh, aren't they beautiful! Are they tame? Can I touch them?'

'Hop out and go over to the fence, they'll come up to you. They're well used to people rubbernecking. This is a new venture also, deer farms. They've run trials at the Agricul-

40

tural College and quite a few farmers have small deer herds.'

Fern found it hard to leave, but when Mr. Alexander beckoned she obeyed ... after all, it was his outing. On towards the hills they followed the road which then turned north and grew narrower as it twisted and turned uphill through some of the most glorious ferns and forest. Now and again Fern caught a glimpse of a lake below them. Once they stopped to admire the exciting beauty of the Dorothy Falls, then on through the bush until they came out suddenly on the edge of a huge lake.

'Drive on down to those seats and we'll stop and sit a while. I never get tired of the view across Lake Kaniere.'

Fern did as she was ordered and then sat on the seats beside the lake with Mr. Alexander, happy that he felt no need to extol the delights of this beauty spot.

After some time they moved once more to the car rather reluctant to leave the scene of unsurpassed beauty, the small islands a short way from the shore and the lake set in, and reflecting, the magnificent bush.

'Just drive on, Fern, we'll come out on the main road in about ten minutes and will soon be home.'

Fern was surprised how quickly the tavern came into view, but pleased too because Mr. Alexander looked very tired, and also her foot was beginning to feel a little sore although she did not have to put any pressure on the wound.

They arrived home in time for afternoon tea. As Mr. Alexander settled into his comfortable chair with a sigh, Brett watched him a little anxiously. 'Did you enjoy the drive, Uncle? Where did you go?'

'We did the round trip to Lake Kaniere and back, and yes, I did enjoy it immensely. There's something very soothing about just sitting by the water. And then I had an attentive listener to my tales of the old days, it was very flattering.'

'The history of this valley could hardly be of much

41

interest to *you*,' Brett remarked, looking Fern straight in the eye.

Fern knew very well that he meant she had been only putting on a show of false interest. 'You couldn't be more wrong. I enjoyed myself thoroughly. Your uncle has a wonderful gift of making people from the past really come alive, as if the horse and buggy days were only yesterday. You probably have grown up with him and not noticed or just accepted it as ordinary, but it gave me real pleasure. Some of his stories should be written down before they're lost.'

Brett's blue eyes challenged her. 'Tell me one that caught your fancy particularly.' He was again implying that she was putting on an act.

Fern flicked her hair over her shoulder, and tilted her small chin. 'I'll tell you two, even though I can't remember the names of the people.

'One was about a young couple driving home from town in their trap, and some of the harness on the horse snapped, and the horse was rearing and ready to bolt. The husband managed to hold the horse just long enough for his wife to get out of the back and grab the baby, which was wrapped in several shawls and rugs, then as the ribbons cut into his hands he let the horse go and jumped clear. They watched the horse plunging madly, and the trap swung from side to side of the road as the crazy animal galloped for home, and only then did the mother look to the baby she was clutching. But the baby wasn't there. She'd grabbed the shawls, and the baby was rolling loose in that awful trap. It isn't hard to imagine how they walked and ran towards their home in fear and terror expecting to find the trap in a ditch or the baby on the road dead. But when they reached their home, the horse was standing in the yard, with the trap still attached and the baby miraculously unhurt.'

Kirsty nodded, 'Yes, I remember hearing about that. Oh, that poor young mother!'

Brett prompted, 'And the other one?'

Fern laughed, 'Oh, it was a horse and buggy one and very funny. A man who owned a very vicious horse which was a notorious kicker also had another failing – he always had too much to drink when he went to town. One night after leaving town he was just sitting letting his horse meander home as usual, and he drifted off to sleep, and when the horse stopped to graze he slipped from his seat and fell behind the horse. He was terrified that the horse would start to kick and kill him if he tried to duck under the shafts, or hoist himself back up on the buggy. So all night long he walked behind his horse pressed hard back against the buggy, and when a neighbour found him next morning he swore he was stone cold sober, and off beer for life. I think that's hilarious. No need for Alcoholics Anonymous!'

They all laughed with her, and the old man beamed on her, knowing very well what had been in his nephew's mind. Not only did he have an apt pupil but one who had the feel for an age that was now gone.

'Brett, fetch Gypsy in when you've had your cuppa. Just put the bridle on for me.'

Brett's attention was now wholly directed towards his uncle. 'A little flattery must have gone to your head. You are not riding today. As it is I think you've overdone it.'

'Who said I was riding? You just do as you're told.' He enjoyed the way Brett stared at him. Do him good to have a few surprises.

'But you never let anyone ride Gypsy but yourself.'

'All I'm asking you to do is to catch her, put a bridle on, and bring her to the house. If I choose to show Fern my mare it's certainly none of your business.'

'That's different. If you want to skite her off, I don't see why you can't wait till tomorrow.'

'I'm not accustomed to waiting.'

Brett stood up and placed his cup on the table, and grinned, 'I'll buy that.'

'Cheeky young whelp!' But Brett had gone. Mr. Alexander relaxed back in the chair and closed his eyes. 'I'll have a catnap, it'll take him half an hour to get Gypsy. Call me when he's back.'

Fern and Kirsty gathered up the tea things and went out to the kitchen. 'You do the dishes, Fern, while I ready up a steamed pudding. Do you know why Mr. Hamish wants the horse?'

Fern shook her head. 'Not a clue. Perhaps he does just want to let me see her. That's if he's proud of her.'

Kirsty sniffed, 'I'm thinking proud isn't the word. He worships that horse. He bred it here on the farm, broke it in himself, and has never let anyone else ride it. I wonder what he's up to.' She busied herself mixing the pudding. 'If you would care to peel the potatoes?'

'Nothing would give me greater pleasure than to be entrusted with such a delicate task.' Then she laughed gaily at Kirsty's disapproving stare.

Kirsty's smile was slow in coming. 'Your parents must miss having you about them. A young girl's laughter is a happy sound in the house.'

'Then you don't mind me teasing you?'

'When I do I'll be letting you know.'

Fern giggled. 'I have no doubt you will!' Suddenly her heart warmed to this stern old lady, and she touched Kirsty lightly on the arm. 'Thanks for letting me help you.'

She left the room quickly, hoping Kirsty hadn't seen those stupid tears brim over, but the old lady missed very little.

As she dropped the last potato in the pot, she saw Brett leading a black horse on to the lawn. She went to call Mr. Alexander, but found him already on his feet. He stopped in the kitchen to get two lumps of sugar, then hurried out to Brett.

Fern followed slowly.

'Ah, my little beauty, have you missed me?' the old man crooned to the horse. 'There now, manners, and you shall

44

have your sugar. There, there. Come, Fern, come and meet Gypsy. Now, tell me if you've ever set eyes on a prettier mare.' His hands petted and fondled the small black horse.

'I don't know much about horses,' Fern admitted honestly, 'but she does seem a darling.'

'She is indeed. Now, Brett, give Fern a leg up.'

Brett gasped, 'You don't mean you're going to let Fern ride her?'

Impatiently Mr. Alexander turned. 'When will you learn to do as I tell you? Toss her up.'

Before Fern could protest she was sitting astride Gypsy. Mr. Alexander instructed, 'Talk to her, pet her, let her know you. That's right. Feel nervous?'

Fern shook her head. She was not frightened of the horse, but dead scared she would do something wrong and upset the old man.

'Now, hold the reins like this, in one hand. See, you've got control, just a touch and she'll turn right or left as you bid her. Remember her mouth is like silk. Don't jerk on the reins ever. Gently, just gently. I want you to learn to ride her bareback, before you get a saddle. Now grip with your knees, get the feel of her. Right, now, Brett, you lead her round the lawn and bring her back.'

Brett did so without speaking one word, while the old man sat on the chopping block watching. 'Sit up straight, Fern. That's right. Take her once more round.'

This time Brett muttered some words under his breath, but he didn't argue.

Back in front of the old man they stopped. 'Thank you, Brett. You can be on your way now. Fern will do very well here on the lawn.'

Brett leaned back against the woodshed. 'I'll wait a minute, just to see if I can believe my eyes. You letting that little hippie actually ride Gypsy, the pride of your heart! She must have cast a spell on you. A few years back and they'd have burnt her as a witch.'

'Take no notice of him, Fern. Now are you comfortable? Just tighten the reins a little, not too much, just a lift, and round you go.'

As Gypsy stepped off daintily she heard Brett say, 'You're going to let her ruin a damn good horse, and probably break her flaming neck into the bargain.'

Fern did not hear what Mr. Alexander answered because she was too busy concentrating on guiding Gypsy around the large lawn. With a feeling of relief she stopped in front of the men.

'Good, grand, you did very well. Don't sit so tense, but keep your knees tight, keep the feel of the horse. Never jerk the reins, even if you're falling, just catch hold of the mane if you want to, or slide off, it's not very far. My word, I can see I'll make a rider out of you in no time! I'll have you riding like a Red Indian. Away you go!'

This time as she started the circuit she heard the parting phrase from Brett, '. . . like a sack of potatoes.'

Fern liked the horse, but found it hard to ride bareback. She didn't want to learn to ride like an Indian. It was not the sort of accomplishment she'd find much use for in the future. However, Mr. Alexander did not seem to be a man who could be lightly turned from his purpose.

After half a dozen trips he held up his hand, and Fern stopped beside him. 'A very good start. Brett, help her down.'

But Fern wasn't going to have any of that, she grasped the mane and slid off, landing with great care on her good foot. Sack of potatoes indeed!

'Watch me, Fern. I'm taking off Gypsy's bridle. See, it's quite simple. You'll do it tomorrow night. Now, give her a sugar lump. Hold it on the flat of your hand. There.' He turned to Brett. 'Gypsy can stay here on the lawn, we'll be needing her each day.'

He walked with Fern to the house. 'We'll have a grand time. I'll let you help Kirsty in the mornings, just to keep her sweet, then we'll go for a drive after lunch, and a riding

46

lesson each night. How does that sound to you?'

'Sounds like a full programme.' Fern was thankful that she didn't have to say whether she thought she'd survive it or not.

younger than I thought. Well, err cheerfully, promise you're not going to make a fool out of myself. He's his . . . she'll

CHAPTER FOUR

DINNER each evening had developed into an amateur debating centre. Brett had given up sitting silently by letting Fern have control of the conversation. Now with careful cunning he probed her views on different controversial subjects: apartheid, the forthcoming tour by the Springboks' Rugby team, the raising of the beautiful Lake Manipouri to supply more power for industry, the New Zealand commitment to Vietnam.

Fern's brown eyes would sparkle with the light of battle as she stated her views, waited for him to demolish them, then they set to, each delighted when scoring a point from the other. Mr. Alexander, his blue eyes alight with mischief, encouraged Fern for all his worth, but it was always Kirsty who scored the final point of any argument. She would listen to each point of view carefully, and as the clash grew more personal, she would suddenly, with a shrewd dry comment, bring laughter and a pleasant atmosphere back to the table.

On Thursday, evening, after Kirsty had dealt her usual coup de grâce, there was silence for a few minutes, then Brett caught Fern's eye across the table.

'Tell me, what do you hope to achieve by drifting around the country?' His tone indicated that he wasn't trying to provoke her, but that he was really curious.

'Do I have to achieve anything?'

'But you must have a goal. What are you looking for?'

Fern laughed, 'I don't know.'

'Then how will you know when you find it?' Brett was genuinely puzzled.

'I'll know,' Fern stated firmly.

'What is it. Money?'

'Definitely not. I may not know what I'm after, but I do

48

know what it isn't.'

'A man?' Brett suggested.

'No. Wrong again.'

Mr. Alexander, who had been watching Fern alertly, asked, 'Perhaps it's security. A place where you want to belong?'

Fern said, with a smile, 'You could be right, but if that's it, I obviously haven't found it yet.'

The old man fingered his beard thoughtfully, then said, 'You like this farm. You show every indication of enjoying the Valley when we're out driving, and get on well with all the neighbours you've met. Would you like to live your life in this district?' He leaned towards her as if to emphasize the next point. 'What would you do if I left you my share of the Matai Valley Farm?'

Fern chuckled, then in mock reproof scolded, 'Hey! I thought you were my friend. That would be a really dirty trick, to lumber me with a great hunk of property. I'd never forgive you, you'd ruin my whole way of life. I like moving on. I want to know what's over the next hill, what's round the next corner. If I was tied in one spot, no matter how lovely, I'd just wither and die. You wouldn't like that on your conscience, would you? Turning a happy carefree girl into a wise and prudent property owner, overcome by responsibilities.'

As she got to her feet to help Kirsty clear the table, she became aware of the peculiar expression in Brett's eyes. She caught her breath. Surely Brett didn't take the old man seriously. Why, that was completely ridiculous.

Next morning as she joined Kirsty in the kitchen, there was a strange car parked in the drive.

'Doctor Walters,' Kirsty answered her unspoken question. 'He often comes out to try for a trout, especially after heavy rain such as we had last night ... the river will be rising. He'll be along to have breakfast with us, I'm thinking.'

She had scarcely finished speaking when the doctor knocked on the door and opened it. 'Good morning, Kirsty.

49

Here's a fine trout for you – eight pounds if it's an ounce. I've got a smaller one to take home with me.' Then catching sight of Fern he asked cheerfully, 'Well, my little anarchist, thrown any bombs lately?'

Fern greeted him happily. 'Not a one. I have to wait for my foot to heal – you've got to be able to run pretty fast, after throwing a Molotov Cocktail!'

Doctor Walters put his fish on the bench. 'I'll have a chat with Hamish while you're preparing my breakfast.'

There was no doubt that he was a frequent and welcome visitor to this house, Fern decided, as she saw him make his way down the passage to Mr. Alexander's room.

When Fern carried in Mr. Alexander's breakfast they were both deep in conversation, but broke off abruptly when she entered the room. When Fern offered to bring his meal in the doctor stood up. 'No, I'll come along with you now. We've finished our discussion. See you again, Hamish, and remember Robbie Burns', "The best-laid plans of mice and men . . ." '

At the breakfast table the doctor chatted away, and Fern enjoyed his visit, even though he could not resist teasing her.

'You disappoint me, Fern. I came out to see a real revolutionary at work, and you've been very slack. I thought the least I'd find would be you marching round with placards, and Ross Smith and Robbie out on strike. Very disappointing!'

After breakfast, he offered to take the stitches out, and thereby save her a trip into town. He was very pleased with the progress of the healing. 'When are you planning on leaving, Fern? I'd like to see it again, say next Friday?'

'Yes, make it Friday. I could see you in town and then head off down to the Glaciers,' Fern agreed.

When he had rebandaged her foot he asked her to accompany him out to the car.

It was a beautiful morning following the rain, a freshness in the air and the warmth of the sun made it pleasant just leaning on the doctor's car. The doctor seemed in no hurry to leave, but Fern felt he had brought her out here to say something, and was taking his time leading up to it.

She picked out the hill she knew now, Mount Graeme, Mount Doughboy, and Mount Camel Back.

'Have you enjoyed your visit here, Fern?' The doctor's voice brought her back.

'Very much. They've been marvellous to me.'

'You won't have any regrets when you leave here?'

'Oh, no. It's been fun. I've learned to ride – not like an Indian, but adequately. I can make Gypsy stop and start, when I want her to, and I can stick on when she walks, trots, or canters. That's not too bad.'

'It hasn't been dull, then?'

'No, really, I've had a wonderful time. Mr. Alexander's a darling.'

The doctor's expression was quizzical. 'He might be, but a very devious one. Do you know why he asked you here, Fern?'

Fern looked at him in surprise. 'Because I got hurt in his car, and he was sorry about it.'

'Oh, the old beggar is a bit deeper than that. Brett tells me you've been getting a crash course on this district, and Matai Valley Farm in particular. Didn't it occur to you that Hamish was laying it on a bit thick?'

Fern smiled. 'No. He loves this place, he knew I was interested and wasn't staying long, so he's been very kind, showing me around.'

The doctor shifted his position. 'How do you get on with Brett?'

'Brett? Well, I guess we don't get on too well.'

'Why not?'

Fern shrugged her slim shoulders. 'You know. He thinks I'm a drifter, a bludger, in fact, I'm the sort of person he disapproves of most.'

'And what do you think of him?' the doctor probed.

'Oh, I can take him or leave him.' She giggled, 'I would

prefer to leave him. Still, that's not fair, I suppose he's not bad. If we'd met under different circumstances, perhaps I might have even liked him.'

'And he might even have liked you, isn't that so? You've been so clever putting on an act that you've never let Brett see you as you really are?'

Fern tossed her long hair back so that she could get a clearer look at the doctor. He continued, 'Did you know that Hamish has a very short time left to live? . . . it could be a matter of weeks, certainly not more than a few months.'

Fern gasped in dismay. 'Oh, I am sorry! No, no one told me.'

'Don't be sorry. He's an old man, and has lived a good life. He's had it hard and he's had it rough, but all in all, I think you could say he's enjoyed it, and achieved all that he wanted, bar one thing.'

'What is that one thing? You don't have to tell if it's personal.'

The doctor looked down at her small heart-shaped face and sighed. 'I think I'd better tell you, so that you'll know what to expect. He and his brother worked very hard, and went without a lot to get this farm, then after the war they took on the next farm when Brett was born. His – Hamish's, I mean – whole life is wrapped up in this farm. He has trained Brett to take over when he dies, but what is occupying his mind to the exclusion of everything else at the moment is who will inherit it from Brett. He wants Brett married.'

Fern wondered why the doctor was telling her all this, as it really didn't concern her in any way, but she said, 'I guess that's a very natural wish.'

The doctor snorted. 'You told me that day at the surgery that you weren't thick, but I'm beginning to doubt your word. Can't you put two and two together? Can't you see the connection between his wish to see Brett married, and your invitation to stay here?'

Fern gaped, then whooped with laughter. 'Oh, no, I won't

buy that! I'm not the one who's thick. Brett and *me*? You've got to be joking. Why, Mr. Alexander knows we're poles apart, and what's more he enjoys seeing us fighting.'

'Of course he does,' the doctor said grimly. 'That's part of the plan. He wants Brett to notice you. If Brett were completely indifferent to your being here, the old devil wouldn't be half as smug as he is. I think you're going to come up against some pretty strong opposition if you try to leave next week.'

Fern was still laughing. 'I'm not taking you seriously, How did you dream this up?'

'Mr. Alexander as good as told me so.'

Fern stopped laughing abruptly. 'Look, I can't believe it, I really can't.'

'You'd better believe it.' The doctor rubbed his hand over his face. 'I'll tell you a bit about Brett, then maybe you'll follow the old chap's thinking. Brett lost his parents when he was very young, he grew up in a house with much older people, he was a lonely little chap, and although Kirsty and Hamish loved him, they were not demonstrative people. Hamish trained and groomed him from a small fellow to take the responsibility of these farms. He was sent to an agricultural college, then spent a year in Britain studying farming methods, then a few months each in Canada and the United States. Brett has never been in doubt about his destiny.'

Fern waited.

'To go back a bit. When he was still in primary school, Mr. and Mrs. Hargreaves bought the farm over the road.' Fern followed his pointing finger, and saw the house further up the road.

'Well, they had a small daughter, Lisa. She was a beautiful child, and grew more lovely as time went on. From the first time Brett and Lisa met, they were inseparable. It was uncanny. I suppose he'd have been eleven or twelve, and Lisa about two years younger. She was blonde, with big blue eyes, and a gentle sweet nature. I guess you could say they

53

were going steady from then on. Lisa went to the local high school, while Brett went away to boarding school, but it made no difference to their friendship. To my knowledge Lisa never went out with any other boy, not that they didn't try to date her . . . she was a real charmer. Then Brett went to college, and she had a job in Hokitika in a lawyer's office. You know, I'm an old fool, but there was something special about those two young people, Brett — tall, slim and dark, and Lisa — blonde and cuddlesome — well, I guess you'd call her sexy or whatever, but it was something to see them together. The old man was pleased as Punch, he liked Lisa; I don't know anyone who didn't. Well, to cut a long story short, Brett went overseas. Mr. Hargreaves had a heart attack, and had to sell the farm, and the family moved to Christchurch. There was no official engagement between the two kids, but it was understood they'd marry when Brett came home from his year in England.'

Fern turned, her eyes following the outline of the mountains. She didn't want to hear what was coming, she felt as if a lump was blocking her throat.

'A month after the family moved to Christchurch, Lisa married her new boss. I still find it incredible, so I don't know how it felt to Brett.'

Fern said thickly, 'How could she have done that to him. What a stupid girl!'

The doctor said sharply, 'Why do you think she was stupid? Because she lost a great chap like Brett? You must like him more than you think!'

Fern faced him, not caring about the tears that rolled down her cheeks. 'Don't you *dare* try analysing me!'

'Certainly not. That's the whole bit anyway. Brett stayed away a year longer, came home and took up the running of the farm. He attends all the local social occasions, but never with the same girl twice. I don't think he'll ever marry — he's twenty-nine now. And Lisa, poor Lisa. Her marriage was a failure, they were divorced last year, but she's a widow now; he died in a climbing accident in July. She has two children.

So it's a pretty miserable story all round. You were brought here by Hamish, to try and stir Brett out of his general apathy towards girls. You couldn't be more different from Lisa if you tried – dark hair, brown eyes, slim as a whip, and there's nothing gentle or sweet in your treatment of Brett. At first Hamish hoped Brett would react against having a girl in the house, sort of shock tactics, but I gather the old devil has fallen for you and you're the one he wants for Brett's wife.'

Doc Walters patted Fern kindly on the shoulder. 'Cheer up, if they get too much for you come into town and see me.'

Fern watched him get into the car. 'I will. Next Friday when I leave here.'

'Cheerio. I wouldn't put my money on that!'

Fern went about her work very thoughtfully that morning. Did Brett and Kirsty know what was in the old man's mind? Somehow she thought not. Kirsty might have guessed, but Brett's manner had not changed since she had arrived here, and she had a fair idea that he would have reacted violently if he had a clue what was going on. Then there was Mr. Alexander himself; he might be crafty, but Fern liked him very, very much. And he did not have long to live. Round and round went her thoughts, dwelling for some time on the picture of the dark lanky boy and the soft cuddlesome blonde. She imagined them riding together, working together, dancing together. Angrily she tried to push the thought of them from her mind. How could a girl who had such a wonderful relationship with a boy hardly wait till he was clear of the country to marry a complete stranger? And now that she was widowed why hadn't they come together again?

She wished that the doctor had not told her anything. She kept reading meanings into words that were probably completely harmless. But Brett had been upset with his uncle when he started teaching her to ride his horse . . . and there was that enigmatic look in his eyes when his uncle had offered to leave her the farm. Oh, she was glad she hadn't known this then, or she wouldn't have been able to act naturally or laugh spontaneously. Now she would be aware of the undercurrents and be watching warily, and she was sorry.

'Where are we going today?' she asked Mr. Alexander at lunch. 'We've just about covered most of the territory: Lake Kaniere, and the Kokatahi Valley, and all the newly brought-in farmland beside Mount Camel Back, and we've been to Shantytown. I do wish I'd been there the day it opened, to see the wedding in the church with the bride and groom and attendants and guests all done up in old-fashioned gear. That must have been fantastic. It's a wonderful idea for a tourist drawcard, the gallows and prison, but of the whole working model of an old-time town. I thought the old printing press was the most interesting.'

She flushed, feeling that she was gabbling, trying to forget what she knew, and talking too much.

'We're off up the Hokitika Gorge today. I'll show you a farm where the chap ploughed up a whole heap of Maori artefacts. Strange how that farm has changed hands several times, but they didn't turn up till now. We passed it the other day, but I forgot to point it out. I don't know if he has them still, we may call and see.'

As they went out to the car Mr. Alexander called to Brett, 'How about coming with us?'

Brett, who had been on his way to the woolshed, retraced his steps. 'You've had a sudden change of heart. Early this week you were adamant that I wasn't allowed to go with you. Now I'm invited. Don't tell me that Fern's flattering attention is beginning to flag?'

Mr. Alexander slammed his door shut. 'If that's how you feel you can stay home. There's no need to be insulting. Drive on, Fern.'

Fern did so, and felt her heart lift. She was right, Brett had no part or knowledge of the old man's scheme. The astonishment on his face when invited to join them was genuine, and genuine also was the quick opportunity taken to say something detrimental about her. Well, that was a relief.

'I'll show you the place where the biggest manhunt in the Dominion's history took place, then we'll go on up to the swing-bridge over the Gorge.'

Fern was quite happy driving, and followed directions until Mr. Alexander indicated that she should park in front of the Kowhiterangi Hall.

'See across the road there, Fern, a neat tidy farm, a bit of a hedge and a square of cement – that's all the visible remains of a house, farm buildings belonging to a man named Stan Graham. He was a fantastic shot and knew the hills and bush around here as well as he knew his own farm, and was fanatical about his physical fitness. It was in 1941 – yes, October '41, that he took his gun and shot four policemen and a chap Ridley who was over at the School. Ridley was Chief Agricultural Instructor for the Canterbury Education Board.'

'Why did he do it? Do you know?' Fern demanded.

'He became mentally unbalanced. Years before the shooting he did several peculiar things, and in the months prior to the shooting he began to believe there was a conspiracy against him. His pedigree bull died and he blamed his neighbour. Anyone who didn't believe his stories became an enemy too. Then he started threatening people with a gun, and that's how the police came into it. After complaints were laid against Graham, Constable Best, who was stationed at Kaniere, and who, by the way, was one of the most popular policemen the district had ever known, came out to see Stan. He tried to reason with him, but was ordered off with a Winchester . . .'

'What did he do then?'

'He went to Hokitika to report to his senior officer, and then those two plus two constables went out to interview Graham. When they arrived he was quite rational, so the police went to see his neighbours to clear up the point about the poisoned cattle. The sergeant was satisfied that Graham was dangerous, so he took his party back to the farm, to confiscate the guns. That must have been the final straw, them wanting to take his guns, so he shot them all, including Ridley, who had come over to see what all the shooting was about.'

'But did he get caught?'

'Oh, yes, they got him all right, but not before he'd shot to death two local Home Guardsmen. For, straight after the first shooting, he packed food, guns and ammunition, and cleared for the hills. For thirteen days he eluded the police, the Army, the Home Guard and local farmers, but then he had all the advantages. He was unknown to most of the hunters, he knew every inch of the country, and he was a first-rate bushman, and a deadly shot. It was dangerous work trying to hunt him down, and it took a while to get all the helpers organized into a co-ordinated unit. Graham came and went in the darkness, and even though he was wounded twice during those days, through the shoulder and through the hand; both turned badly septic – so he must have suffered torment – but he was carrying two fully loaded guns when they shot him down. He was a tough man.'

Fern said, 'It seems funny I've never heard about it before.'

Mr. Alexander replied, 'Well, don't forget it happened during the war, and before you were born, and people don't talk about it much, preferring to forget it happened. All sorts of myths and stories sprang up afterwards, some even trying to make a hero out of him, sort of one man pitting himself against organized society, but he wasn't that, he was deranged and a killer.

'They even say Lord Haw-Haw from Germany announced that a cable had been sent to Graham saying, "You hold the South Island. Hitler sending another man to hold the North." I suppose it sounds funny, but to people living here at the time, there wasn't much humour in the situation.'

'Sounds a bit like Ned Kelly, or Jesse James,' Fern suggested.

'Maybe, but let's drive on to the Gorge now. I'll sit in the car while you climb the bush track to the swing-bridge. It's not far, and the colour of the water sixty feet below the bridge defies description.'

On Sunday Fern went to church with the family, and they were joined by Smithy. Brett drove and the three women sat in the back. Fern, being on the opposite side of the car to Brett, for the first time studied him objectively. He had a good profile, a strong face; add to that his thick dark hair and neat sideburns, and she had to admit that he wasn't all that unattractive ... all right then, he was attractive ... but definitely not her type.

Fern wore the tunic top of her brown crimplene trouser suit, and highly polished boots on her slim legs. She had had to reduce the bandage to get them on, but it wouldn't hurt for one hour. With her hair caught back with a brown chiffon scarf, she had presented herself for Kirsty's inspection before leaving. The tunic was very mini indeed, and Fern felt Kirsty wavering between 'indecent' and 'neat and tidy', and was quite elated when 'Neat and tidy' prevailed. If she stayed long enough she might get Kirsty into a mini, or maybe – no, she wouldn't. Kirsty looked every inch a lady in her midi-length navy blue dress, with a froth of lace at the neck. Fern wouldn't like to change her.

The week passed very quickly. Fern was busy learning to work in the milking shed. She now rose at five and enjoyed the hour and a half with Ross and Robbie. Robbie was a real nut, always doing the wrong thing. The comical grin he wore when bawled out by Ross amused Fern, but only added to Ross's rage.

On Thursday morning as she was going home from the cowshed, Brett caught up with her. 'Can I have a word with you, Fern?'

'Sure,' Fern answered. She was in a happy mood this morning, and Brett's request had been unusually politely spoken . . . that is, for him.

He did look a bit diffident, which was also unusual, being normally so sure of himself that it verged on actual arrogance. 'Please put the milk billy down. This will take a few minutes.'

Fern did as she was asked and waited.

'You're supposed to be leaving tomorrow?'

'Not supposed to be leaving, I am leaving tomorrow,' Fern said flatly.

'Would you reconsider your decision? I would like you to stay on for a while, if it doesn't interrupt your plans too much.'

'Why?' Fern asked suspiciously.

'I know I've got a neck asking you for a favour, Fern, but I have to ask.' He was embarrassed.

'Why?' Fern was determined to be unhelpful. 'Don't tell me you can't do without my charming company?'

'I could do very nicely without you. Whoops – sorry, that wasn't very diplomatic. I'll come straight out with it. My uncle has taken a great fancy to you. He hasn't long to live. Since you've been here it's as if he'd found a new lease of life. I know it's temporary, but I would do a lot to keep him happy, if only for another couple of weeks. Then there's Kirsty. She's devoted to the old devil, and she's been feeling the strain of these past few months a great deal. She flatly refused to let me get her help in the house, not even Smithy for an hour a day, and yet she quite likes Smithy. But she actually seems to enjoy sharing her work with you.'

'Incredible! Fancy anyone enjoying being with me!' Fern snapped.

'Well, will you stay for their sakes?'

'Not for yours? Oh, I am disappointed!' Fern teased wickedly.

'Yes, in a way for me, because if they improve because you're here, it's all I want.'

Fern suddenly relented. It must be hard for him to beg a favour from her. 'Very well. Nobody is going to be waiting for me anywhere, so I might as well be here. If it comes down to tintacks, I've grown rather fond of Mr. Alexander and Kirsty myself. I'll stay another two weeks.'

'Thank you very much. I'll make it worth your while,' Brett said gratefully.

Fern bent down and picked up the billy. She was so angry she could hardly speak. 'You mean money, I presume?'

Brett, walking beside her, was unaware of the storm he had unwittingly stirred up. 'Yes, of course. You said you take odd jobs here and there. Well, I'd be happy to put you on the payroll.'

'How much?' Fern snapped.

He looked at her in surprise. 'I don't mind how much, just as long as you'll stay. Say a hundred dollars?'

'Say three hundred,' Fern hissed. 'What price do you put on the comfort of your family?'

Shocked, Brett stopped. 'Why, you cheap little chippie ... well, not cheap! Lord, I'd love Uncle to see his pet hippie putting on the squeeze!'

Fern's normally brown eyes were nearly a black-brown. 'And as you don't trust me an inch, and I don't trust you, I'll have it in advance, today.'

'You can damn well have a cheque right now!' Brett stalked ahead of her.

By the time she had put the billy on the table and had a wash, he was waiting for her, cheque in hand. He thrust it out. Fern took it and examined it carefully, while Kirsty watched the two of them in surprise.

Fern looked him straight in the eye. 'I guess it won't bounce.'

'You sweet little ...' He stopped himself by sheer will-power. 'It will be honoured at the bank.'

Fern took the cheque in both hands, and carefully ripped it into tiny shreds, then threw them in the incinerator. 'I don't take pay for helping my friends. To me, friendship is priceless. How dare you offer me money?' The tears spilled over. 'Don't keep breakfast for me, Kirsty, I've lost my appetite. I'm going for a ride on Gypsy.'

Fern rode along the ridge in front of the house, then galloped along the farm road to the creek at the back of the farm. She lay on the bank and cried her heart out. This must be the 'blues' that the staff nurse had warned her about. She just felt terrible and didn't know why. When she was sure Brett would have left the house she cantered home, and let Gypsy go, glad that she had found a lump of sugar in her pocket.

She turned around to go into the house, and there was Brett standing directly in front of her. She went white and moved to pass him.

'No, you don't.' His hands gripped her shoulders. 'You'll stay here while I apologize.'

'To hell with your apologies!'

'Fern, listen to me.' He spoke forcefully. 'I'm deeply sorry that I offended you. It was quite unintentional, and not meant to insult you. I was a crass idiot.'

'And damned stupid to boot!'

'I agree. Insensitive and stupid. Will you accept my sincere apology?'

Fern sighed wearily. 'Yes.'

His hands dropped from her shoulders. 'I'm glad. You're a strange girl, Fern. I've never met anyone quite like you.'

'I'll buy that, there isn't anyone quite like me.' It was a feeble attempt at a joke to show that the quarrel was over.

He smiled at her. 'Generous, too. You will stay?'

Fern felt her colour rise at the compliment. 'Yes, I said I would. I'll go inside now. Too much drama on an empty stomach isn't good for one.'

She was conscious of his eyes watching her until she entered the house.

CHAPTER FIVE

As Fern entered the roomy kitchen Kirsty put her rejected meal on the table. 'Eat it!' she was ordered brusquely. 'I've had enough trouble with Brett. I'm not here to cook meals that are not eaten. I'm thinking you two should spend some time in a country where people are starving. It would give you some appreciation of good food.'

Fern set to the meal with a will. The ride had given her a rare appetite, and strangely she felt much happier than she had done when she had been up at the far creek.

'What about Mr. Alexander's breakfast?' she asked.

'Are you thinking that I would let him starve while you two are gallivanting over the countryside?'

Fern saw that Kirsty had also been badly upset by the performance in the kitchen. Perhaps she was still worried. 'I'm sorry about this morning, Kirsty. I misunderstood Brett, and thought he'd been rude to me. He met me when I came back from my ride, and apologized. It's all fixed up now.'

Kirsty's face relaxed, and she smiled, just a little. 'I'm glad; Brett apologized? I'm thinking that must have been a new experience for him.'

Fern laughed with her.

'Now what can I do? The polishing?'

'No, I've got an important task for you. One of my hens is laying away from the henhouse. I'm fairly sure her nest is in the barn, but I can't find it. There are quite a few bales left over from the winter feeding, and each time I go in the wretched bird sets up such a clamour and squawking that I don't know where she's appeared from. Now if you go over and crawl on top of the haybales and be very quiet, you'll find what I'm missing, maybe. It will be a long wait, perhaps.'

Fern grinned, 'I've always wanted to be a private eye, now I have my chance! I'll stalk her with all the stealth of a professional shadower.'

'Just lie still and quiet. That's all that's required, but no doubt that will be hard on such a restless body as yourself.'

Fern went over to the barn and climbed to the top of a stack of bales. It was cool and dark out of the sun, in this high, spacious barn, and Fern lay full length so that she could see Kirsty's wandering chook when she appeared, yet would not be seen herself.

She had been there quite a long time when Brett and Mr. Alexander walked in. She did not say anything because she thought Kirsty would have told the old man what she was doing, and as she didn't know from which direction the hen would come she didn't want to scare it off. To her dismay she saw Mr. Alexander take a seat on a box by the doorway in the sunshine. She wished they'd get going, or they'd make her job impossible. It wasn't until they had been talking a while together that she realized she was eavesdropping on a very confidential conversation, and by then it was too late to move.

'It was hard. I don't think you young ones have any conception of the sheer physical hard grind that farming was in those years. No tractors, all the work done by horses, no front end loader and trailer, just pick and shovel, no insecticide to kill the gorse, but a grubber and an aching back; that, my boy, is the way your father and I cleared this land.' He waved his hand impatiently as Brett went to speak.

'I know you've heard this all before, time and again, but listen now. You know I've a short time left, and it will be all your's, and I'm well pleased that it should be so. It's always made me proud to have you with me, and to know what your father and I sweated and worked for isn't going to be lost. But when you get to my age, who are you going to pass it on to? You're twenty-nine, most of the boys you grew up with are married and have children about them. Are you going to live single all your life?'

Brett squatted down beside his uncle. 'Look, we've been over this before. I'll marry when I'm ready and not before.'

'Have you anyone in mind?'

'No.'

'Are you still fretting about that silly boy-girl affair you had with Lisa?'

Fern heard the weariness in Brett's voice. 'You know I'm not.'

Mr. Alexander relentlessly pursued his goal. 'She's a widow now. If she's the only one for you, I wouldn't stand in your way. She would be welcome here with her children.'

There was pain and anger in Brett's response. 'Lay off, can't you. It was more than a boy-girl affair, as you call it, and you damned well know it. I loved Lisa for ten years, I trusted her, I thought I knew her as well as I knew myself. Do you think I'd have her back again? I'm not stupid. Once trust is gone, there can be no question of love.'

'Well then, marry Fern.'

Fern gave a startled gasp.

Brett shouted, 'Now I know you must be mad! Why should I want to marry Fern? We've nothing in common.'

'Does that matter? You say you'll marry some day. You're getting on. There's no one in the district to suit you. You can't have Lisa, or don't want her. Then why not Fern?'

'Because, for one thing, she wouldn't have me.'

Mr. Alexander snorted impatiently. 'How do you know she wouldn't have you? You haven't asked her, have you? You haven't even been decent to her. If you set out to win Fern, I'm sure you'd succeed.'

'But I don't want to. It's as simple as that, get it. I don't know one reason that would make me want to marry her, or anyone else, for that matter.'

'That's the whole point of this argument. It doesn't matter to you which girl you marry, so why not Fern? I want to see you married before I go. I won't put it more strongly than that. And if you do choose Fern, I'd be very happy, and somehow I think you would be too.'

Brett stood up and stretched. 'What makes you say that?'

'Because I know Fern, I know her a lot better than she thinks I do. She's like your own mother in character. If you managed to win her love, you'd have a wife in a thousand. She's a fine girl, and will grow into a fine woman. She has integrity, and a loving heart, and if you don't take up the challenge, you're a damned fool.'

Brett helped the old man to his feet, and had one last word. 'You call her a girl? She's a woman, she's twenty-four, so that's how well you know her. I saw it the day I checked on her driver's licence.'

'Will you promise to think about it?' The old man had lost his aggressiveness and was pleading now.

'I'll promise to give it some thought, and that's all.' Brett left the barn, and after a few minutes so did Mr. Alexander.

Fern lay quite still. Poor old man, he wasn't going to get his last wish. Poor Brett! To have lost the girl he loved, and yet could not bear to think of taking anyone else for his wife.

Suddenly a hen squawked right beneath her, almost startling the life out of her. She watched the cunning chook come out from a hole between two bales. Fern hopped down to find the nest of eggs, then she set off triumphantly to tell Kirsty, 'Mission accomplished.'

At lunch time Mr. Alexander was missing, and Kirsty said he was in bed and wanted nothing to eat. When Fern half rose to go to him, Kirsty said, 'It's best to be leaving him alone for a while. Have your lunch, then see if you can cheer him up.'

When Fern knocked on his door, and went in, she was shocked to see the change in him. He was tired and his colour was bad.

'Would you like some lunch now, Mr. Alexander?'

'No, nor do I want a cup of tea, I've already told Kirsty so. I don't want to be fussed over.'

'You don't feel well enough to take our planned trip to the greenstone factory, or the tour of the big milk powder plant?'

'No. Go on your own – Brett will probably let you have the car.'

Fern replied, 'Let's cancel it. It wouldn't be any fun if you weren't with me. Could I just sit here and talk to you? Or would you like me to read a book aloud?'

Mr. Alexander seemed to shrink down into the bed. 'Please leave me alone. Go away.'

Fern walked away sadly. Out in the garden she spoke to Kirsty, offering to help her.

Kirsty shook her head. 'You go off and visit Mrs. Smith, or go for a ride.'

Fern wandered off towards Smith's, only to find them dressed up leaving for town. It just wasn't her day. Too much had happened. She strolled across to the cowshed and visited the calves in the calf paddock for a while, then looked over to the gravel pit which was full of water and saw the newly hatched grey ducklings taking their first swim. They were darling little balls of grey fluff, swimming along after their mother. Fern laughed as she watched them.

From a short distance away Robbie called, 'Come and give a hand.'

Fern joined him. 'What are you supposed to be doing?'

Robbie leaned on the grubber. 'Hard labour!'

Fern laughed. 'Doesn't look too hard. Give it to me.' She took the grubber and leaned on it. 'See, nothing to it?'

'Very funny! You're supposed to chop out all the ragwort ... see that green weed with the yellow flowers? It's all pretty pathetic really, because we'll be boom spraying it with weedkiller next week. It's just Ross's way of getting at me. He's been on me back all week. I've a good mind to go and find him and tell him to keep his flaming job.'

'You'll have a long walk. I went to visit Smithy, and they

were leaving to go to Hokitika.'

Robbie stared. 'Why didn't you say so straight away?' He gave a bloodcurdling Tarzan yell, and twirling the grubber over his head three times, let it go sailing through the air. It landed close to the edge of the pond. 'Come on! It's a lovely afternoon for sitting in the sun, doing nothing, and more fun if you've got a pretty bird beside you.'

Fern followed him protesting, but Robbie took no notice, so she sat down beside him.

'Now cheer me up!' he commanded. 'I've had a rotten week, and stuff your conscience with the thought that all work and no play makes Robbie a dull boy.'

'Oh, so that's why you're dull! I wondered!'

'I'm not getting through to you, I can see that. You're to flatter me and build up my ego, which has had a sad thrashing. Lay it on real solid.'

Fern smiled. He did actually *look* unhappy. 'Robbie, I think you're *so* handsome, and wise and intelligent, and I'm sure you have such a marvellous personality that you have to carry a can of insect repellant to keep the girls off. Will that do?'

Robbie ran his fingers through his curly hair. 'Not bad at all. I'm beginning to feel better already. I think you could do better if you tried harder. How about – you appeal to me because you're . . .'

'Such a nut,' Fern finished.

'I guess I am.' He lit a cigarette. 'I lost my bird last weekend and got stoned, and nearly lost my job because of it. If Brett hadn't stepped in Ross would have sacked me. You know, you often hear people say, old so-and-so, his bark is worse than his bite . . . well, with Ross it's different.'

'I like Ross,' Fern said indignantly.

'I might too, if I was a pretty girl, and he fell all over me to make a good impression,' Robbie said dolefully.

'Tell me about your girl.'

'You mean tell you about the one I had last week? Her name is Maureen, and she's . . . aw, what's the use? She got mad because I had a few drinks too many and she went home with another bloke. So I went on to enjoy what was left of the party, which wasn't much after she'd gone, only the booze. Well, I got a rare skinful and someone dropped me off at the gate. I navigated the drive successfully, and was just going to walk in the door, when I fell over the wheelbarrow full of wood. It made a bit of a noise, enough to wake the dead, Ross said. Well, he blew his lid. He's not what I call a charmer at any time, but at three o'clock in the morning, he's out of sight.'

'Not quite,' Fern laughed.

'Sunday morning, all stations were go. You weren't in the shed, unfortunately, or he may have had something else to occupy his tiny mind. After lunch I'd promised to help clean up the hall where the party was held, and there was Weird Harold chatting up Maureen, so I went out the back and cleaned up what was left in the keg. I didn't get home to milk, because someone brought another keg from somewhere, and so it was a repeat performance of Saturday night.'

'Not the wheelbarrow, I hope?'

'Do you think I'd be stupid enough to come in the front door twice? No, I decided to avoid the wheelbarrow by coming in the back door. I would have made it too, if some great steaming twit, who shall remain nameless, hadn't decided to leave the wheelbarrow strategically positioned at the back door steps. Do you want me to go on?'

Fern shook her head.

'I should think not! The language that old buzzard used hasn't been heard here on the Coast since the bullock waggon days.' He picked up a stone and threw it close to a pair of paradise ducks which were swimming past.

Fern remonstrated, 'Don't do that! They're so nice, they haven't hurt you.'

Robbie growled, 'Anybody or anything that looks happy hurts me. What right have they got to enjoy life? There's a party on this Saturday night, and Maureen won't even speak to me. I've phoned her and each time she hangs up before I can get a word in.'

'I think I'll go and see how Mr. Alexander is.' Fern got to her feet.

'Hang on a minute! I've just had a brainwave. How about you coming to the do with me? If Maureen saw me with a smashing-looking bird like you she might have second thoughts.'

'Thanks, but no, thanks. I'm far too old for you, Robbie, and have far too much sense to try making a girl jealous. It wouldn't work.'

Robbie was on his feet. 'What are you going on about? I'm twenty-one, I'd be years older than you, and I promise not to drink, and I'll forget about making Maureen jealous. If you don't come with me, I can't go, all the others have jacked up their partners ages ago. Aw, come on, Fern!'

'If you'd promised Maureen not to drink you would be going with her,' Fern said. 'I'm twenty-four.'

Robbie roared with laughing. 'Who do you think you're kidding? Anyway, how can I promise Maureen anything when she won't speak to me? Say you'll come. It'd be a real gas.'

Fern hesitated. Robbie smiling was irresistible, but Robbie downcast and begging was even more so. 'Yes, I'll go with you, but if by any chance you manage to convince Maureen that you're prepared to lead a sober and upright life, for her sweet sake, then count me out. I mean, I'm all on Maureen's side. No girl wants to get all partied up and then have a boy breathe beery fumes all over her – that is, if he's capable of standing.'

Robbie's lopsided grin was back in place. 'I knew you couldn't risk missing some action. Twenty-four, huh! If you're that old I'm Gary Cooper.' He picked her up and swung her round in a circle.

As Fern regained her feet she said sternly, 'Any more of that, and you can find yourself another partner. And remember, I'm just as fussy as Maureen. If you take me out and get tight, I'll see that Ross hears about it, if I have to go over and tip over the wheelbarrow myself.'

'No. Scout's honour. Lips that touch wine shall never touch mine, and all that guff. I feel so good I'm going back to work. Shows you what the influence of a good woman can do!'

Fern went home to help Kirsty prepare dinner, then rode Gypsy to bring in the cows for milking. She helped about the cowshed enjoying the soothing sound of the pulsation of the milking machines. She still hadn't got used to the sight of the cows lining up like angle-parked cars.

When she'd showered and changed for dinner, she found Kirsty quite upset, but endeavouring to conceal it. 'Mr. Alexander won't get up for dinner.'

'I'll take it in to him,' Fern offered.

'No, he says he can't eat.'

'I'll go and talk to him.' Fern went quickly down the passage. The door was open, so she walked in. 'Kirsty says you're not joining us for dinner. I wish you would. I need you.'

'What do you need me for?' His tone showed no real interest in her reply.

'I had a row with Brett. Oh, he apologized, but I'd like you there to sort of give me moral support.'

His eyes brightened. 'Brett apologized? What did you fight about?'

Fern said, 'I'll tell you if you get up and have dinner with us. Here's your dressing-gown and slippers.' She felt a bit mean as she saw the hope come back into his face. She helped him up and said, 'It wasn't really much of a row, but it upset me.'

'Tell me,' he urged.

'It was rather silly really. Brett asked me to stay on for another couple of weeks. I said I would, and he said he'd put me on the payroll if I'd stay. I was mad. He didn't have to pay me to stay.'

'No, no, he was very stupid. Brett asked you to stay?

71

Hmm, that's good. Hurry now, we mustn't keep Kirsty waiting.'

Fern knew very well that Mr. Alexander thought Brett had asked her to stay after the talk they had had in the barn. It was wrong of her to lift his hopes; but she hadn't told a lie, it was the timing which was of paramount importance. Still, anything was better than seeing him lying in bed so miserable and defeated.

As they sat down to dinner Brett said, 'You'll be pleased to know that Fern isn't leaving tomorrow. I've asked her to stay on for a while.'

That was all that was needed to put Mr. Alexander in high good humour. He ate his meal, listened to Fern telling about seeing the new grey ducks, and laughed heartily at her humorous account of Robbie's trials.

It was only as dinner finished and Fern said that she was going to the party with Robbie on Saturday night that she realized she had lost all she had tried to gain.

Mr. Alexander stood up. 'I'm glad that Robbie doesn't let slip the chance of taking a pretty girl out. Shows the boy has sense, more than some people I know.' He glared at Brett. 'I'm going back to bed.'

He stayed there all day Friday and all day Saturday, refusing to take his meals, refusing to talk to Kirsty or Brett, and being barely civil to Fern. Fern wavered between being angry with the old fellow for putting such pressure on Brett, and admiring him for fighting for what he wanted, using the only methods he had at his command.

Fern went to see him before she left for the party on Saturday. She was wearing the same greeny-brown trouser suit as she had worn the first night at dinner in his house.

'Delightful, my dear, truly delightful. I hope you have a very happy time.' But there was no sparkle in his eyes, no real interest.

The hall was artistically decorated with huge king ferns and tubs of flowers. Fern was more interested in the band that played such toe-tapping music.

One dance with Robbie convinced Fern that no matter how catchy the music was her foot was not going to take too much abuse. She was quite happy to sit and watch the others and listen to the music . . . well, happy wasn't quite correct. She would have much preferred to spent the evening at home with Kirsty, but she had promised Robbie, and she was stuck with it. She knew that the vivacious redhead was Robbie's Maureen, and it rather amused her to have the girl casting oblique glances at her from time to time. She saw the partner Maureen had with her, and thought if that was 'Weird Harold' then Robbie needn't worry about the competition too much.

'Go and ask her for a dance, Robbie,' Fern urged. 'I'm sure she would accept. She's been looking over here hopefully, just waiting for you.'

'Well, she can wait.' Robbie was extraordinarily stubborn. 'She made me sweat it out all this week . . . see how she likes it. If I leave her long enough with that drongo, she'll fall on my neck when I start my search and rescue attempt.'

'Go and dance with someone else, then. You don't have to babysit me.'

'You wouldn't mind?'

Fern shook her head, and was quite relieved when Robbie took off across the room to join the group around Maureen. She saw the affronted expression on Maureen's face when Robbie partnered the girl standing beside her on to the floor. He came back to Fern to report progress, and the next dance took the girl the other side of Maureen.

It didn't bother Fern how he sorted out his difficulties, as long as she could go home soon.

'Hullo, Robbie abandoned you?' Brett sat down beside her.

It was silly to be so pleased to see him. 'I wasn't expecting to see you here. You didn't say you were coming. And Robbie didn't abandon me, I chased him away. You see, I can't dance, and anyway, I only came with him so that he would have a chance to get his bird back.'

'Would you like to go home?' Brett asked.

'Oh, I'd love to go home, but I'll have to wait till Robbie makes what he calls his Search and Rescue attempt. I wish he'd get a move on.'

While Brett lit a cigarette she said, 'Don't feel you have to keep me company . . . I'm fine on my own.'

'I prefer to sit here, not for your sake but for my own. I guess I'm not in the party mood.'

It was only then that Fern saw the lines of strain on his face. It must be really eating into him, that he could not carry out the task his uncle set him. Being a nurse she knew what weight relatives put on a dying person's wishes. It wasn't fair. Compassion for him welled up inside her. She felt like putting her hand on his arm and saying, 'Ask me to marry you, and I'll turn you down. That way your uncle's anger will be directed at me.' But she couldn't say that . . . she wasn't supposed to know what was troubling him.

Robbie joined them, and his mood was one of barely concealed triumph. 'Next dance and she's mine!'

Fern scoffed, 'I wouldn't count my chickens before they're hatched. She hasn't got that red hair for nothing. If you'd played with me as you're doing with her I'd have seen you dead before I'd dance with you.'

'That's why she's my girl, and you're not,' Robbie grinned unrepentantly.

'That's one of the reasons. The other one is I wouldn't have you gift-wrapped.'

'Hey, Fern! You *are* packing a punch. What's the matter? Has Brett been needling you?'

'No, you are. My foot is hurting, and I want to go home, so either you fix things up with Maureen now, or I'm going over to tell her what you're playing at, and then see if you get anywhere with her.'

Robbie beat a hasty retreat, and the next dance he was on the floor with Maureen.

Brett touched her arm. 'Is your foot really painful?'

Fern smiled. 'It is a bit, but not nearly as bad as I made

74

Robbie believe.'

As the dance finished Robbie brought Maureen to the table to introduce her to Fern. They only stayed a few minutes, then Robbie said, 'I told you, Maureen, that I was only taking care of Fern till Brett came, and you didn't believe me. You've got a nasty suspicious mind, and I'll expect you to be extra nice to me tonight to make up for having such wicked thoughts.' As he walked away with Maureen on his arm he turned and winked at Fern's outraged face.

'The sneaky little beast, dropping me in your lap as soon as he's got what he wants! Well, that young man's in for a surprise. I'll go and sit in his car, and he'll know all about the saying "two's company, three's a crowd" before this night's out.'

'He's aggravating, I'll give you that, but you're the one who'll suffer most if you wait for him. This shindig could go on for two or three hours. Do you think your anger will sustain you all that time? I'm off home now, you're welcome to a ride.' Brett stood up waiting for her.

Fern decided to go with him. She could always catch up on Robbie tomorrow.

When they arrived home Brett garaged the car, then remembered that Fern was only wearing light sandals, and the ground was muddy from the rain over the past two days.

'Hang on a minute,' he walked round the car and scooped her up into his arms and carried her across to the cement, put her down carefully on the garden seat, then sat down beside her. Fern sat there thinking of the last time he carried her along the hospital corridor. She had been so furious that she had promised herself, if he ever picked her up again, she'd bite him if there was no other way to retaliate, yet now she felt no anger.

'It's a beautiful night.' She sighed, thinking that the beauty of the night wasn't going to help Brett with his problem. She watched the huge full moon, rising over the mountains, casting its silvery light along the willows and pine trees, touching everything in its path with magic. She felt the anger and frustration in the man sitting beside her, but could not think of anything to say to help him, so she just went on sitting there, feeling somehow that he was glad of her company.

'You're very quiet.' Brett spoke at last.

Fern quoted, ' "To everything there is a season, and a time for every purpose under heaven ... a time to keep silence and a time to speak".'

'What's that from?' Brett looked at her.

'The Bible, you know – Ecclesiastes, Chapter Three, "A time to be born, and a time to die; a time to weep, and a time to laugh; a time to mourn and a time to dance." That's not in the right order. When I was away at boarding school whenever the principal was out for blood she read that out at prayers. I suppose that's why it sort of stuck in my mind.' Fern stood up. 'I think it's time to go to bed now.'

Brett stood up too and looking down at her, said, 'You're a strange girl.'

'And you've said that before.'

'I wish I'd know you when you were at school.'

Fern laughed, 'You wouldn't have liked me. I was pretty revolting, in more ways than one.'

'The worst girl in school?'

'No, that was my best friend. The principal once said to her, "If you were twins we'd be forced to close down the boarding establishment!" '

Brett put his hands on her shoulders. 'You seem no more than a child during the day, running around barefoot in those scruffy pants, then in the evening, like now, you suddenly grow up.'

He took one hand from her shoulder and gently smoothed her hair back from her face. He stroked the length of her hair, and Fern stood quiet under his ministrations. They couldn't be called a caress.

He spoke again. 'I've watched Uncle do that; your hair has a fascination for him, it's so thick and luxuriant. I've never admired dark hair before!'

His hand tightened on her shoulder until it hurt. 'That old devil is going to lie down and die on me. What can I do?' He suddenly released her. 'Sorry, did I hurt you?'

'No,' Fern lied. Her heart really ached for him. It was stupid, she wasn't involved with these people. She could walk out of here tomorrow if she wanted to ... couldn't she?

He cupped her face in his hand and kissed her lightly. 'Go to bed, Fern.'

She hurried inside, and it wasn't until she was tucked up in bed that she let the tears fall. Was he going to go along with his uncle's wish?

Mr. Alexander had challenged Brett to make her fall in love with him. At the time she had thought it was not worth bothering about ... but now she wondered if he really set his mind to it, would she be able to resist him?

On Sunday morning at breakfast, Kirsty had given up all pretence of hiding her feelings. 'Brett, I'm worried. He just lies there and refuses to eat. You've tried, I've tried, and Fern has tried, and still he won't eat. I think we'll have to call Doctor Walters. You know what that means, he'll have to go to hospital. I can't go to church. I can't leave him.' Her voice shook.

Brett, his face stern and his chin set at a stubborn angle, said flatly, 'He knows what he's doing. Leave him one more day, Kirsty. We'll call the doctor in the morning. And you have to go to church. I can't remember you ever missing church.'

'I'll stay with him,' Fern offered. 'Don't worry, I've had a bit of work in hospitals; I'll know how to handle him. Don't be surprised if he's sitting up dressed and waiting for his Sunday dinner when you come home.'

Kirsty glanced at her doubtfully. 'Honestly, I've never seen him like this before. He seems to be shrinking away before my eyes ... I'm thinking he wants to die. I never thought I'd see the day that Mr. Hamish would give in.'

'He hasn't given in, Kirsty.' Brett's voice was grim.

When they all left for church, Fern tidied up the kitchen, and prepared the vegetables, after she had put the roast of beef in the oven. On Sunday only they had dinner at midday, the rest of the week the main meal was in the evening. Then she went down to Mr. Alexander's room.

'Are you going to get dressed ready for dinner?' Fern asked cheerfully. 'It's a lovely day, and I've put a chair out in the sun for you.'

'I'm not getting up. I wish you would leave me alone.' His voice was still very strong.

Fern moved around the other side of the bed so that he could not avoid seeing her. 'That's exactly what I'm going to do. If you don't come out with me now – I mean, get dressed and sit and talk to me, and have dinner with me – I'm going to get my pack on my back, and I'll leave as soon as the others get home from church.'

Mr. Alexander glared at her. 'You said you would stay another two weeks.'

'Yes, but only because Brett convinced me that I was good company for you, and a big help to Kirsty. So if you won't have anything to do with me, I'm off.'

'You mean that?' The old man was incredulous.

'I surely do.' Fern felt mean. She did not like indulging in emotional blackmail, but the thought of Kirsty and Brett at the breakfast table strengthened her resolve. She would play the old man at his own game.

For some minutes it was touch and go. Then, 'Get out of here, girl, while I get my clothes on.'

When she got back out to the kitchen, Fern let out a sigh of relief. She felt as if she had just finished a hard shift on duty. That old man was indomitable, a real tiger. But even he could see he would have lost the game if she left.

When the car drove in from church, Mr. Alexander was sitting in his chair in the sun, dressed in his navy blue Sunday suit. Fern was kneeling at his feet, reading a book aloud to him. She saw the look of relief on Kirsty's face as she came towards them, and felt like warning her not to be too pleased. Fern had doubts that because she had out-manoeuvred Mr. Alexander this time, she had won. She was sure that his brain was busy working out another form of attack.

She was right. Mr. Alexander sat with them at lunch but refused to eat. If anything it was worse than when he stayed in his room. He was keeping to the letter of the agreement, but not the spirit. So she had accomplished very little indeed.

After lunch Brett surprised Fern by asking, 'You got any-thing on for this afternoon? I thought you might enjoy a drive somewhere?'

Fern hesitated, looking towards Mr. Alexander, who shook his head, and said, 'Not me. I'll stay here and keep Kirsty company. You two get along.'

Fern was already dressed in a dark green pleated mini-skirt and yellow top, and she hurried to her room to pull on her calf-length boots. Now that she did not need such a width of bandage on her wound. The boots were very comfortable. She let her hair swing free, knowing that if the occasion arose it would make an effective screen to hide her thoughts behind. What made her think she would want to hide her thoughts?

Once in the car she tried to relax and pretend it was an ordinary outing, but all the time she knew it wasn't. She knew that Brett had come to some decision ... there was a sureness in his manner that had been missing last night. Not that it made her feel any easier. If he tried to pretend he had fallen in love with her, she would never forgive him. That kiss last night, had it been the start of his campaign?

He must have felt her gaze, because he looked directly at her. 'Enjoying the drive?'

'Er ... yes.' Fern blushed as if he had been reading her mind. She had been so preoccupied with her thoughts that she had not even taken note of the direction in which they

79

were travelling. Only now she noticed that they had left the tarsealed road and were travelling along a gravel track, through native forest.

Soon Brett pulled the car off the track and parked. They got out and Fern followed him along the edge of a swift mountain stream. After a short walk they came to a natural clearing in the bush, and Brett sat down by the creek. 'Well, here we are, in the sun and out of the wind, and more important, no one is likely to disturb us here.'

'Where are we?' Fern asked. She could not recognize any of the mountains she had become familiar with, although that was not strange, because when she had been out driving with Mr. Alexander she had noticed that even Mount Camel Back became unrecognizable from certain angles.

'Does it matter?' Brett inquired, his blue eyes watching her intently.

Fern shrugged her shoulders. 'No, I guess not. It's nice here. There's a good bushy smell, sort of cool and dank, but not unpleasant. I can see a lancewood, a rimu, some bush lawyers, and what's that bird calling? A tui?'

'This isn't a field trip to identify the natural fauna and flora. I brought you here so that I can talk to you. Sit down somewhere, you're giving me a crick in my neck.'

Fern chose a smooth flat rock a little distance away, and folding her hands in her lap, said, 'I'm listening.'

'What did you say to Uncle to get him out of bed? It must have been something pretty drastic.'

'It wasn't,' Fern protested. 'I just said that if he didn't want me around I'd leave.'

'No wonder the old devil made such a remarkable recovery.' Brett was silent for a time, then suddenly, 'Have you ever been in love?'

Fern jumped. 'Yes, half a dozen times . . . well, I thought it was love, but it wore off in a few weeks or months, so I guess it was infatuation. It seemed real enough at the time . . . sounds a bit weak really. They say love is a chemical reaction. I think someone must have left out the essential ingredients ... my romances all start with a bang, and then go out like a damp squib.'

'So you haven't got a steady boy-friend at the moment?'

'No, I've no one really special.'

'That makes two of us. There hasn't been anyone special for me for a long time. Once long ago I was very much in love with a girl, but she married someone else.'

Fern thought she couldn't bear to hear that story again, so she said, 'I know, her name was Lisa.'

Brett glanced at her, his expression unreadable. 'I should have known someone would tell you ... Smithy, I suppose?'

Fern did not correct him. There seemed no reason to bring Doctor Walters into this.

The sun had moved and now Brett's face was in the shadow. She was about to ask him what he was leading up to, when he started speaking again.

'You seem to be very fond of Uncle Hamish. According to Doctor Walters he hasn't got a lot of time left; he has cancer, and as if that wasn't enough he has a clot travelling round his body. If it reaches his heart or brain death will be instantaneous.'

'Embolism.' Fern spoke involuntarily.

'Yes, that's the correct medical term. How did you know?'

'I told you I worked in a hospital for a time,' Fern replied defensively.

'Ah, yes, I forgot. Anyhow, his chances of seeing this summer out are mighty slim. Naturally if he has to go I hope the clot takes him off. At least that will be quick, with no prolonged suffering.'

There was a long silence, then Fern sighed, 'Why are you telling me this?'

Brett sat up, but his face was still hidden from her. 'Fern Fraser, will you marry me?'

It took Fern's breath away. How dared he ask that, with

no more emotion in his voice than if he was asking for a second cup of tea? Why was she shaking when she had been half expecting something like this ever since they left home? At least he was honest. She had to admit that. He had not pretended warmth or affection which he did not feel. She stood up. 'Thanks, but no, thanks. Why me?'

'Why not? Uncle Hamish thinks you'll make me a good wife, Kirsty says you haven't a lazy bone in your body, and Robbie thinks you're a smashing bird.'

'And what do *you* – think?' Fern demanded. 'Do you think I'd make a good wife?'

'I don't trust my own judgment on the subject of women and matrimony. I was very wrong once ... this time I prefer to leave the choosing to others.' The pain and bitterness were naked in his voice.

'Fern moved to the edge of the stream, watching the water rushing downhill, bubbling and chattering on its way to the river. 'You say I'm strange; I haven't got that all on my own. No man would let someone else choose his wife ... no man could be completely indifferent to a decision that would place a woman by his side for the rest of his life, the most intimate of all relationships. Well, I've never met one yet.'

'You have now. I only care deeply for two people, Uncle Hamish and Kirsty. You can take it or leave it; the offer is there.'

The bleakness in his voice caught at Fern, making it impossible for her to speak.

She sensed he was close to her, then his hand rested on her shoulder. 'Don't let it worry you. It was worth a try, even if it was only to make Uncle's life more pleasant for a couple of months. Oh, well, I did my best. Come on, let's go home.' He turned towards her, and looked at her closely. 'Why, you're crying. Who for? You? Me? ... or maybe Uncle Hamish?'

His arms went round her, holding her not tightly, but comfortingly. 'Just forget all about it. I was stupid to mention it. I knew there wasn't a hope in hell of you accepting me.'

Fern brushed away her tears, leaning back in his arms so that she could see him, she said, 'Sorry about the crying, I've only been doing it since the accident. I do like your uncle. I would like to make him happy. Couldn't we have a pretend engagement? he wouldn't know the difference. I'd like to do that much for him. And I would be a help to Kirsty.' Fern was thinking that being a nurse, she might be able to take care of Mr. Alexander at home, keep him in his own beloved surroundings a little longer.

'But you won't marry me?'

'No, I don't mind a pretend engagement, but I couldn't have a pretend marriage. I just couldn't.'

'What big eyes you have, grandma!' Brett smiled down at her. 'Then it's settled, we're engaged, and we'll buy the ring tomorrow. But remember, to me an engagement is a binding contract leading to marriage. You can pretend all you want, and pull out when you're ready, but for me it's for real.'

Abruptly he pulled her close and held her, then his lips came down on hers, not lightly this time, but in a hard, compelling, demanding kiss.

Fern pulled away from him, angrily rubbing her mouth. 'What did you want to do that for?'

He laughed, mockingly. 'I hope I didn't offend you, thought it was quite in order to kiss you now that we're engaged. After all, we can't continue sniping each other across the table. You'll have to agree with me now and be sweetly charming and loving.'

Fern backed away from him. 'Drop dead! If you think I'm going to drip honey all over the place just because I'm wearing your ring, you're in for a horrible shock. And don't kiss me again. We only have to pretend when there's someone round, not when we're alone. Is that clear?' She was desperately trying to regain control of the situation which, in her opinion, was getting badly out of hand.

'I'll go along with anything you say, *dear*!'

He was laughing at her. Infuriated, she turned and hurried back to the car. As she sat waiting for him to come her hand went to her mouth again. It was quite ridiculous to be upset about the kiss. She had been kissed before, hadn't she? Well, this had been *different*.

Brett did not keep her waiting long. As he got into the car he asked pleasantly, 'Do we break the news when we get home or save it until we get the ring tomorrow?'

'Tomorrow.'

Brett laughed again. 'Sufficient unto the day is the evil thereof! or something. Tell me, what did Doctor Walters say about your foot on Friday? I should have asked before, but things have been kinda hectic.'

'It's all right,' muttered Fern, and was furious when her face flushed crimson as she remembered Doctor Walters' parting sally. 'See you in church!'

CHAPTER SIX

MONDAY morning began badly and became worse as time passed. There was nothing dramatically wrong, just a hundred and one things joined together to frustrate and annoy everyone.

Fern decided against going over to the cowshed, so that she could get a good start on the washing. She stripped down the beds and changed the bed linen, then put out all her clothes on the bed ready to sort out those she wanted to wash. Before she could do so, Kirsty called her.

'Fern, Robbie's just been over with a message from Ross, he wants you to give a hand, apparently they're running late or something.'

'Blow! I wanted to do the washing, I've quite a lot of my own stuff to put through.' Nevertheless she hurried to put on her gumboots and went over to the cowshed.

Joining Robbie in the pit, she asked, 'What's up? Anyway, I've been waiting to have a word with you about Saturday night . . .'

Robbie rolled his eyes. 'Just leave it. By the time Ross has finished with me, even you wouldn't be so rotten as to have a piece of me. Well, that's if I'm still alive when he's finished.'

'Where is he?' asked Fern, as she worked alongside Robbie.

'If you look at the yard you'll see there's only half the herd here. I put the dog around them as usual, but someone, a fisherman probably, had left all the gates open after we put them away last night. So when I herded them, half headed for home, and the other half took off for parts unknown. I tried to get them back for half an hour, but the dog decided he'd had enough and cleared for home. I could hear Ross roaring from the far gate and so brought these on down. His language was so lurid that the grass around me started to smoulder. Thank God his batteries had run flat by the time he got to me, and he just had the strength to whisper, "Get Fern to help you," and stalked off towards the river.'

Fern looked towards the back of the farm. 'Here he comes now, so shouldn't you open a gate or something?'

Robbie scowled, 'The old buzzard can open his own gates. I'm not going to stick my neck out after the way he explicitly described my ancestors this morning.'

Fern hurried out and followed Ross's signals. The errant cows entered the concrete yard with a shamefaced air, somewhat similar to children who have been caught playing truant.

Ross, his face a pale shade of puce, muttered, 'Glad we've got someone with a few brains.' It didn't help his temper to find that six of the cows had mastitis, which meant they had to be milked separately and treated with penicillin, making the milking process even longer.

As Fern finished feeding the calves she saw Brett riding behind a mob of Hereford steers which he penned in the cattleyards. She knew he was sending a truck of fat steers to Addington to be sold next day. Then she noticed he was bringing a black and white cow and calf towards the shed.

When Ross came out of the shed Brett called cheerfully, 'Didn't know you had any cows calving this late, Ross? Something gone wrong with your family planning programme?'

Robbie, who had been helping Fern with the calf buckets, put them down hastily. 'I'm splitting this scene . . . you will too if you've got any sense. You can tell Ross I've gone to put the cows away. When he explodes the fall-out can be more damaging than that from a hydrogen bomb.'

By the time breakfast was over the truck driver had arrived and Fern had to make a fresh cup of tea. She had only finished clearing that one away and washed the breakfast dishes, when a local farmer arrived to ask help of Brett, who was president of the Federated Farmers, so another cup of tea was made, and another half an hour later when a stock and station agent called. Mr. Alexander demanded her attention until it was time to put lunch on.

As they finished lunch, Kirsty was angry to hear rain pounding on the roof. 'Fancy, I'm thinking that I had no need to rush through the washing. But it's only a spring shower, and will clear away soon.'

Brett caught Fern's eye across the table. 'I'm going to town immediately after lunch, would you like to come with me?'

It was only then that Fern remembered that they were to buy the ring today. She went to her room to change, and found to her horror that Kirsty had collected all the clothes off her bed, and they were now hanging wet and limp on the line. She could either wear the distinctly grubby jeans she had on or the only article left in her pack ... a pair of thoroughly disreputable shorts and a torn shirt which she had intended to discard. It wasn't so bad, because she had intended to buy some new clothes today when she was in town. She put her faded frayed shorts and shirt on, brushed her hair till it was shiny and glossy, and went out to the kitchen carrying her shoulder bag and boots.

Kirsty glanced at her with surprise. 'You're never going to town in those rags?'

Fern laughed, 'I've got no option ... you've washed everything else I possess. Don't worry, I was going to buy some new gear today. I've got my Post Office Savings Bank book with me. Where is Brett?'

'He's waiting out in the car,' Kirsty said. 'Oh, I am sorry I've put you in such a difficulty, I thought you'd left them all for the tub.'

The rain had cleared away as suddenly as it had arrived and the sun was shining brightly as Fern joined Brett.

Brett opened the door for her and then stared. 'I'll wait while you go and change.'

Fern shook her head. 'Sorry, but you take me like this, or not at all.'

87

Brett stiffened, and his blue eyes were cold. 'Oh, I see, an ultimatum.' His arm barred her entrance for a moment, then he said, 'Get in.'

As they drove off, Fern began, 'I can explain . . .'

'Save your breath,' Brett cut in. 'I even put on a collar and tie thinking the occasion somewhat important, while you deck yourself out in clothes that wouldn't be accepted in a CORSO collection. I would prefer you to leave it at that.'

Fern shrugged her shoulders. If that was what he thought, he could carry on. She didn't let his anger upset her, she was busy planning her new wardrobe. Seeing she was going to stay here for a couple of months, she would need quite a few additions. While she had moved on every three or four weeks her few good clothes were enough for the odd evening out, and her jeans or shorts and tops were all she needed during the day. But with Kirsty making her change into a dress each night she was heartily sick of the few changes she had.

Brett drove over the rail crossing and passed the clock tower, then braked suddenly in front of a jeweller's shop.

Fern looked at him in surprise. There was no doubt that he was in a towering rage; his face wore that closed bitter expression which had been absent for the last few days, and his hands were still gripping the wheel so tightly that his knuckles showed white. 'You are still prepared to become engaged to me?'

'To pretend to become engaged to you,' Fern replied sharply.

'Good. I take back the bit I said about considering an engagement being a binding contract leading to marriage. I thought it didn't matter who I married, but I find the thought of being permanently tied to someone as hard and unforgiving as you makes me shudder. There's nothing soft or feminine in you. You dressed with the deliberate intention of humiliating me. It must give you exquisite satisfaction to know that you can make me bend enough to take a scruffy object like you into that shop buy a ring to put on your finger, and introduce you to my friends. If it wasn't for that fact that I'd do anything short of murder to please Uncle Hamish, I'd toss you out on the street this minute, which is all the treatment a little tramp like you deserves!'

Fern's face was white, as his remarks slammed into her like physical blows. Then her small chin lifted. 'What makes you think I'll let you off the hook when your uncle dies? I might sue you for breach of promise?'

'Sue away! I'd be happy to pay up to my last penny, to be well rid of a plaster like you.'

Fern was shaking so badly she could hardly speak. 'I have s-s-some sh-sh-shopping to do. You can go in there and buy the cheapest ring that you can get.' She pulled off her friendship ring from her right hand and laid it on the seat. 'That's my ring size. If you want me to go in with you, I'll be back here in an hour.'

She got out of the car still clutching her boots, and limped down the street to where she had seen the Post Office. So he was humiliated and ashamed to to be seen with her, was he? Well, she'd show him! She'd spend all the money she'd saved during the past six months, and buy herself a heap of ultra-respectable clothes, and she'd act like a lady to please his rotten, stuffy friends, but she would never forgive him for his remarks . . . not ever.

After drawing her money out, she wandered about the streets until she saw a display in a window, a full-length dress in Lincoln green. It was very simple, a scooped neckline, with shirring at the waist, and again on the cuffs of the long sleeves. The material was crêpe, just what she had in mind. She went into the shop, and took a packet of pantyhose from the hosiery bar. When she paid for them, the little shop assistant asked, 'Is there anything else?'

'The green dress in the window?' Fern suggested.

The girl's face lit up with enthusiasm. 'I knew that wouldn't last the day. It's gorgeous, I'd love it myself, but it's not my colour. Green makes me look as if I'm sickening for something, but it would be smashing on you.

Fern followed her into the large fitting room, and taking off her awful shirt and shorts she put on the new panty-hose and her boots, then eased into the long dress. She twisted her long hair into a soft knot at the base of her neck, and looked in the mirror.

'Golly, you look super!' the little assistant said happily. 'I knew you would. Like something out of *Vogue* magazine. You look a bit like Twiggy, with your small face and huge eyes.'

Fern laughed, 'I'm not a bit like Twiggy, at least I can wear a strapless frock if I want to, without having to put a notice on "Front" or "Back"!'

The shopgirl giggled. 'But you are going to take it? It would be a sin not to. I'm not just saying that to get a sale. Really, you look marvellous.'

Fern couldn't help feeling warmed by the girl's admiration, and she did like the dress. 'Yes, I'll take it, and lots of other things if you have them. Could you bring in, say two pair of denim shorts, these have had it, and perhaps two pairs of stretch trews, or hipsters, and a few tops.'

It took Fern no time to choose what she wanted; she was surprised at the wide selection brought for her approval, the clothes were as up-to-the-minute as any city store could provide.

'Now, I'd better have a slip, because I want three or four summer shifts, sleeveless and plain, you know what I mean?'

The little salesgirl seemed to be getting as much fun from helping Fern as if she was getting them herself. She came back with the slip, and an armful of dresses. Fern soon sorted out a gold silk mini, a leaf green tunic-type dress, and two colourful cotton shifts.

'I didn't bring you any midi ones, because it would be a shame to wear them and cover up your legs. Is that all now?'

Fern was still wearing the green mini. 'No, I'll have a

look myself now, if you'll pack those things. I want something smart and sophisticated, but not too way out . . . I'd better just have a hunt around, and I want some new undies too.'

Fern moved along the lines of dresses, pant-suits, and began to feel she was being difficult to please, but she couldn't find the outfit she wanted . . . it had to be special.

The salesgirl was back. 'Can't you see anything that's just right?'

Fern answered with a smile. 'Well, really any of these would do, but I wanted something a bit different.'

The girl flushed. 'Look, we have a smashing suit out the back, it's a bit expensive, though. A customer ordered it, but she was in this morning and she was a bit too f— I mean, the suit was a bit small. I just thought of it because it would go with your bag and boots. It's cream and brown, and there's a cream and brown stetson to go with it. Would you like to try it on?'

Fern tried it, and it was a perfect fit. She pinned her hair higher, and put the stetson on . . . exactly what she wanted.

'Here's gloves to match. Miss O'Brien hunted them out this morning.' The salesgirl helped her put them on. 'Golly, you look super!'

When Fern heard the price she nearly asked for a chair to sit down in while she made wild calculations to see if she had enough. She had, but with only five dollars to spare, after paying for her other purchases. While she carefully made up her face, the shop assistant put all her things in a large carton. Fern stepped back from the mirror – yes, she could face Brett in these clothes. But she would add one more thing, a pair of huge sunglasses. He wasn't going to see how much he'd hurt her.

'Can we put these in your car for you? They're a bit heavy for you to carry far.'

'Thanks very much,' Fern answered. 'You've been a marvellous help. If you'd put them in that red Holden across the street, I'd be grateful.'

'You mean the one Brett Alexander is leaning on?'

'Yes, do you know him?' Fern asked in surprise.

'Everyone around here does. He's a big wheel in this town.'

'Well, you tell that big wheel Miss Fraser will be along in a few minutes.'

Fern went next door to the chemist's shop and bought the biggest pair of dark glasses she could find. It was only when she tried them on that she realized that she'd fought with Brett and that she had not cried. She must be getting better.

She crossed the street to where Brett was standing talking to two ladies. Slipping her arm through his, she said silkily, 'Brett darling, aren't you going to introduce me to your friends?'

The look of surprise followed by reluctant admiration that came into Brett's eyes was worth every cent the suit had cost her, Fern thought savagely.

'Sorry, Fern. I didn't see you arrive. Mrs. Hamilton and Jane, I'd like you to meet my fiancée, Fern Fraser.'

Hiding behind her dark glasses. Fern could almost imagine he sounded proud as he accepted their congratulations. 'Thanks very much, both of you. You're the first to know, and we're just going in to buy the ring, so I hope you'll excuse us?'

Jane Hamilton was staring at Fern intently. 'Hey, you're Fern Fraser! I mean the one that went to St. James' School in Christchurch. Take those wretched glasses off so that I can have a good look at you.'

Fern obeyed with a grin, and found herself hugged and kissed by an ecstatic Jane. 'Why, you mad darling, why didn't you let me know you were on the Coast? Mother, you've heard me speak of Fern . . . you know, her father, Dr. Fraser, is often on TV giving lectures. Oh, Fern, this is fantastic – I mean, you're going to marry Brett and live in the Valley.'

'Fantastic,' agreed Fern, as she replaced her dark glasses. She knew Jane had come from the Coast, but it was a big province, and she hadn't given her a thought. She still didn't know whether to be glad or mad that she had run into her.

Mrs. Hamilton was pressing Brett to allow them to put on an engagement party for them. 'Sorry, Mrs. Hamilton, but Kirsty and Uncle Hamish will want it at home. It was good of you to offer, thank you. Now, if you'll excuse us, we must be getting along.'

He caught Fern by the hand and led her firmly into the jeweller's shop, while she turned to wave a hurried goodbye. At least they would be convinced that Brett was in love with her, dragging her willy-nilly into the shop to put the ring on her finger. Young Lochinvar has come out of the West, I don't think, Fern thought bitterly.

Brett led her through to a small room behind the counter. 'I took the liberty of narrowing the choice down to five or six, that I thought you might like, but if they don't suit you, just say the word.'

The shop owner came through and placed the beautiful rings on a table in front of Fern; with a tactful murmur he withdrew and left them alone. Fern tried on one ring after another, in complete silence. She knew at a glance that they were all exceedingly expensive rings, and she did not want a diamond ring. 'Diamonds are forever' and this was only pretence. Suddenly weary of the whole thing, she said, 'Does it have to be a diamond?'

'It is customary,' Brett said slowly.

'Oh, by all means let us follow custom and convention. You choose – after all, you're paying for it.'

Brett hesitated, and then took a ring, a diamond solitaire. 'I like this one. Do you?'

She was about to answer scathingly, when she saw the owner hovering in the doorway. 'Why, darling, that's wonderful! We both like the very same ring – what a good omen for our future. May I wear it now?' She slipped it on her finger, and picked up her gloves. That would save him the embarrassment of wondering whether he had to kiss her or not. She walked out to the counter and noticed the owner had collected the rest of the rings. As Brett joined her, the owner offered them his congratulations and best wishes. Fern felt the tears spring to her eyes. 'I'll wait in the car, darling,' she said as she made a hasty escape.

The car was locked, but by the time Brett joined her she had herself under control again.

As they drove homewards, Fern was pleased that Brett did not wish to talk; somehow she felt drained of all emotion. She feasted her eyes on the unbroken view of the mountains ahead, feeling somehow more comforted when she recognized Mount Graham, then Doughboy, and finally Camel Back. Silly to think of them as the hills of home.

Brett broke the long silence. 'You didn't tell me that you knew the Hamiltons.'

'I didn't know they lived here. Somewhere on the Coast could be anywhere. Wasn't it fortunate that they didn't see me in my CORSO collection rejection outfit? Think how humiliated you would have been. But I can tell you this, that Jane would still have launched herself on me. One day you'll grow up and learn that you can't tell a book by its cover, nor can you tell a person's character by the clothes they wear,' Fern said bitingly.

'I'd like to say how attractive you look in that suit, Fern, and . . .'

'And nothing. Remember you don't have to be pleasant or polite to me unless we have an audience. Is that clear?'

'Quite clear,' Brett said stiffly. 'But one more thing I must say. You bought a lot of clothes today. Am I right in thinking you wouldn't have needed them if you hadn't been staying on here at my request?'

'Quite correct.'

Brett hesitated, then, 'Would you allow me to pay for them? I didn't mean to have you out of pocket over this idea.'

'I'd rather walk around stark naked than let you pay for

94

my clothes! And I didn't stay here for your sake, but for your uncle's welfare. You owe me nothing, I owe you nothing, and that's the way it's going to stay.'

The rest of the trip was made in angry silence. When they arrived home Mr. Alexander and Kirsty were in the lounge.

Brett took Fern's hand and led her forward. 'Look what I got in town, Uncle Hamish – a brand new niece for you. Fern and I are engaged.'

Mr. Alexander was wildly excited, insisting that they have a drink to celebrate the occasion immediately. He admired Fern's ring and patted her hand. 'There now, that's the most sensible thing you've done for a long time, Brett. I hope you two will be very happy.'

Watching him, Fern could not judge whether he was aware it wasn't a genuine engagement or not. He appeared to be taking it at face value. But Kirsty was not; she eyed Fern keenly, then leaned forward and kissed her on the cheek. 'You're a good girl, Fern.'

Somehow that small compliment made Fern feel much better. Kirsty knew what was happening and why, and she approved.

'What do you think of my new suit, Kirsty?' Fern laughed gaily and struck an exaggerated modelling pose.

'Very neat and tidy.' Kirsty's grey eyes twinkled. 'I'm thinking you should be thinking you should be thanking me for washing all your clothes, so that you had to buy more, whether or no' you needed them. You look fine.'

Mr. Alexander roared with laughing. 'You take that compliment and frame it, Fern, Kirsty is very sparing with praise.'

Kirsty went out to get more cups, and Fern felt Brett take her arm in an iron grip. He led her to the window, out of Mr. Alexander's hearing. 'Why didn't you tell me Kirsty had washed all your clothes?'

Fern glared at him from behind her glasses. 'And spoil your favourite exercise?'

95

'What exercise?'

'Jumping to conclusions, darling!' she said loudly, so that Kirsty looked up, startled. Fern giggled; poor Kirsty wasn't so sure now.

As they had their cuppa, Mr. Alexander was full of business arranging the date of the engagement party, and was angry when he couldn't have it the following Saturday. 'Why not?'

'Because it's a housewarming, for young Joe and his new wife. I was talking to Mrs. Hamilton about it. It will have to be the following Saturday.'

'Huh! What's Mrs. Hamilton got to do with it? Do you mean to say she knew of your enagegement before us?'

Brett hastened to assure him that as she had met them going into the jewellers, he could do little else. 'Did you know Jane Hamilton and Fern were at school together in Christchurch?'

The old man took the bait. 'Well, she'd know your family, Fern. We must invite them down here. Do you think they'd come for the party?'

Fern shook her head. 'No, I know they wouldn't. Could you leave my family out of it, please? I don't want them.' Things were going to be difficult enough without getting her family involved.

'That's right, I remember. There's something odd about your parents, you wouldn't let us ring them when you were hurt. Funny lot, not caring about a sweet girl like you.'

Kirsty interrupted, 'Brett, if you've told Mrs. Hamilton, you and Fern had better rush over to Smith's. Mrs. Smith wouldn't forgive you if she wasn't first with the news.'

'You're right, Kirsty. Come on, Fern, we can't start our married life with an enemy in the house next door!'

He held her hand on the way over to the new house, even though she protested violently. 'Smithy has sharp eyes, and I may even have to kiss you to convince her.'

'You just dare, and I'll slap your face!' Fern warned him.

'They would think you're a little prudish to resist so fiercely when you've got my ring on your finger.'

'Purely temporarily,' Fern muttered.

As they came out from the trees, Brett caught her in his arms and laughed down at her furious face. 'We've got a full audience — Smithy at the window, Ross on the porch, and Robbie at the gate. One kiss now will be more convincing than a hundred of your synthetic "darlings".' He kissed her not at all gently, and as her free hand came up he caught and held it. 'If you do, I'll kiss you again.'

Fern's hand dropped. 'I hate you!'

'What makes you think that's news? Come on, the reception committee is staring open-mouthed with astonishment. Remember, convince Ross, Smith and Robbie, and they'll have it all over the Valley by tonight, but you'll have to try a little harder to cast me a loving glance, or they'll pick it's a jack-up. Why, Fern, you're blushing!'

Fern stiffened. 'I am *not* blushing! I'm angry.'

Brett laughed. 'Why? Did you find my kiss more enjoyable than you care to admit?'

As his guess was perilously close to the truth, Fern replied coldly, 'At least, having an inferiority complex isn't your hang-up. You really are something else. For your information, I think I'd prefer to be kissed by Uncle Hamish than by you. But definitely.'

Brett put on a mock-humiliated expression. 'You really know how to hurt a guy.' Then looking at her outraged face, he threw his head back and gave a great shout of laughter.

Fern watched him in amazement. He was really enjoying himself, and he looked years younger. Come to think of it, she hadn't heard him laugh before. Well, not really. It seemed that by becoming engaged, they had swopped sides; he was acting quite irresponsibly, and she was becoming prim and not a little waspish.

She didn't speak as he took her hand and led her up the path and into the house. She knew she had to pass this test with flying colours. One hint that theirs was a convenience engagement and Smithy would have it all around the district, and it wouldn't be long before Uncle Hamish was told. So she entered the house with a gay smile on her face, and happily accepted their surprised congratulations and best wishes, proudly showed her ring, and did not forget to smile up at Brett with an adoring look on her face. That was the hardest part, when she felt like giving him a swift kick on the shin to take that pleased, almost smug, look of complacency off his face. He was really putting on a fantastic performance, she thought she ought to nominate him for an acting award – say, for Best Supporting Actor, or something.

Smith was so excited and obviously overjoyed that she made Fern feel utterly hypocritical as she said, 'Oh, you two have picked today to announce your engagement just to please me. It's our twenty-fifth wedding anniversary today, our silver wedding anniversary. I was trying to nag Ross into taking me out to dinner at a posh hotel, and do you know what the wretch said? He said he didn't celebrate his failures! Now I ask you . . .' Smithy ended up laughing.

Robbie, standing close to Fern, muttered, 'Told you he was all heart.'

Still laughing, Smithy swooped on Fern. 'Still, he's not too bad really. Come through and see what he gave me for a present.'

Fern went eagerly, glad to be away from Brett in his present mood.

Smithy opened the bedroom door proudly. 'See – a new carpet and this gorgeous bedroom suite. I'm really thrilled about it. The old one we bought second-hand when we married, and I love this modern style. What do you think of it? Sit down and try the mattress.'

Fern was relieved that she could at least be completely honest and lavish with her praise. 'So Ross isn't as tough as he likes to pretend?'

'Oh, he's a real softie.' Smithy's face was flushed with happiness. 'He's been a wonderful husband to me. And Brett will make a good husband too. I can't tell you what it means to me to see him lighthearted and laughing. He's been almost like a son to me, and I hated to see him growing more serious, almost bitter as the years passed. That Lisa had a lot to answer for . . .' Smithy put her hand to her mouth, as if to catch back the last words.

Fern smiled, 'Don't feel embarrassed, Smithy. I know all about Lisa.'

Smithy relaxed. 'Now, that's good. If he could tell you about Lisa, it means that he's at last got over her. He can't take his eyes off you, Fern, he's very much in love with you, that's easy to see.' She was silent for a moment, then, 'Please, Fern, don't hurt him, I couldn't bear to see him lose you as he lost Lisa.'

Fern felt the tears sting her eyes. Smithy was a darling, a loving cheerful person, and she was genuinely anxious for Brett. 'I promise you, Smithy, that I won't rush off and leave to marry someone else. If I leave here, it will be when Brett doesn't need me any more.'

'Thank you, Fern. I guess that won't be for many years, if ever. He even looks younger. Wait a minute.' Smithy left the room quickly, leaving Fern to think how strange that she and Smithy had both felt that Brett had really shed his age. Then she suddenly found the answer, he was relaxed and happy because he had managed to please his uncle, without actually getting himself tied down.

Smithy was back with a box in her hand. She handed it to Fern with an air of satisfaction. 'Bet I'm the first one to give you an engagement present.'

Fern felt awful as she unwrapped the box and lifted the lid. Inside she saw an attractive Pyrex dish. She hadn't given a thought to receiving gifts, and she would certainly upset Smithy if she refused. She thanked Smithy, and thought with dismay, how difficult life had become. Still, she could leave it behind when she left. Brett would see it was returned. 'Yes, it's our very first present, I must go and show it to Brett.'

99

As they left the bedroom, Smithy said, 'I've had a letter from Lisa asking if she could bring the two children here after Christmas for a month to get them out of the city for the school holidays. I was going to refuse her, but now Brett has you, I'm going to tell her she can come. Do her good to see what she missed, and how Brett has found someone to love. You're so much better for him, and I bet he knows it. Lisa is one of those beautiful brainless females, a real clinging vine, whereas Brett needs someone who can stand on her own feet, and also be a help to him in times of trouble.'

Fern went straight to Brett, showing him Smithy's gift, and as he added his thanks to hers, he put his arm lightly round her shoulders. Fern stiffened, and just stopped herself from shrugging his hand off. Only a few more minutes to go before they could make their escape. Then Smithy told him of Lisa's pending visit, and Fern felt Brett's hand tighten painfully on her shoulder. So Brett still loved Lisa! And Smithy, burbling on happily, had no idea that she was going to hurt him badly by bringing Lisa and the children here.

She moved towards the door with Brett's arm still around her. She heard him say, 'Well, that's set. You'll all come over after dinner for drinks.'

Ross replied heartily, 'We'll all be there with bells on.'

Robbie grinned, and then said hesitantly, 'Will it be all right if I drink your health in lemonade? I promised Maureen I wouldn't take a drink for a month.'

Brett laughed, 'You can drink it in anything you fancy, Robbie.'

But Ross turned on him with scathing sarcasm, calling him all sorts of a fool to let a girl boss him around like that when they weren't even engaged. She'd really wear the pants when they got married. He ought to make a stand right now, and on and on about it being an insult to Brett and Fern ...

Robbie, white-faced, left the room, and Smithy turned on Ross. 'What did you upset the boy like that for? There's no pleasing you. You were talking about getting rid of him because he drank too much, now Maureen is straightening him out you've got to lead off at him.'

Fern slipped out from under Brett's arm. 'Do you mind if I talk to Robbie?' When Brett nodded she went out the door and ran down the path to catch Robbie as he let the dogs go.

'Hi! Don't be mad at Brett and me – we weren't to know it would cause a fuss when we invited you over for drinks.'

'Brett's okay,' Robbie muttered.

'What about me?' Fern coaxed.

'You'll do.' Then he looked at her. 'Don't know why you've got to wear that gear for, you look like one of those toffee-nosed twits that get their photos in the papers after the races. You know, Miss So-and-So looked simply *divine* in her purple, pink and red striped outfit, and wearing a face to match.'

Fern giggled, 'Robbie, I love you!'

'You don't, you love Brett. I know I'm irresistible to women, but really, now that you're engaged I think you should try and keep some control over your feelings. If you don't behave I'll tell Brett what an embarrassing time I have fighting you off every time you get me alone.'

Fern was pleased that Robbie was returning to his natural zany self, pleaded, 'Please don't tell him, Robbie, I wouldn't like him to know that he was my second choice. Look, can I ring Maureen and say it's a special occasion tonight? She might give you a special dispensation, or whatever.'

Robbie looked at her with a most un-Robbie-like seriousness. 'No, Fern, but thanks. It's just that she's got uptight about my drinking. Her father was an alcoholic, and she plain doesn't believe me when I say I don't worry if I drink or not. Her father must have been a real brute, whenever he got drunk he'd beat up her mother, and often Maureen and her kid brother. She thinks that anyone who drinks is going to end up the same way. So I said I could go a month without a drink, and she took me up on it. If you ring her she'll be all the more sure that I'm just using you for a cover; and that I'm going to end up like her old man.'

'And what happens at the end of the month? Do you have to become teetotal for life?'

'No, just one month and then I'll start again – I mean just social drinking. I've got to admit, I've made a bit of a pig of myself since I've been over here. It won't cause me any pain to cut back a bit. But if that old buzzard keeps needling me, I'll hang one on him, even if I lose my job. It would be a real pleasure.'

'I don't think he'll bother you ... Smithy was tearing a strip off him when I left. And I'd back her any time. So we'll see you tonight?'

'Sure. Hope I haven't caused a blight on your best day. Brett's O.K., but I reckon he's dead lucky getting a smashing bird like you. No kidding.'

Fern said with a smile, 'Thanks, Robbie. And seeing compliments are flying, I've got to say I think Maureen's lucky too – not many boys would be so understanding about her worries. And remember, if Ross kids you, just stay loose ... See you.'

When she reached the car she found that Brett had taken all her parcels inside. She was going to give Kirsty a mannequin parade. When she went inside Brett was sitting on the table watching Kirsty work. 'Oh, I've put all your shopping down in your room, Fern. Do you think you could spare me half an hour or so, I'd like you to help me move some stock.'

Fern looked at him suspiciously. Ross often asked her to help, even Robbie wasn't above ordering her about to make his work easier ... but Brett had never asked for her help.

'I wanted to show Kirsty my new things,' Fern protested.

'Kirsty will be too busy to see them. She's just rung Smithy to ask them all over for dinner.'

'Well, I'll have to stay and help her get things ready,' Fern replied with relief.

Kirsty said firmly, 'Go and change out of your good clothes, Fern. I don't need your help. Mrs. Smith insisted on doing the sweet course, so I haven't much extra to do. Anyway, a man likes to get his girl to himself sometimes.'

Fern walked slowly to her room. She didn't want to spend any time with Brett alone. She was also angry with Kirsty for leaving her no excuse to dodge going with Brett. So she chose a daring pair of hot-pants and put on a man's shirt in bright yellow silk. She hung up her suit, and put her hat away, then brushed her hair out free, and put on her dark glasses. She glanced in the mirror. Kirsty wasn't going to 'call this gear neat and tidy!'

Out in the kitchen, Kirsty looked her up and down. 'Have you nothing on but that shirt?'

Fern grinned, then pulled up her shirt. 'Hot-pants!' she said wickedly.

Kirsty shuddered, 'Horrible! I'm thinking they were not very generous with the material when they made those, whatever they are.'

'Hot-pants,' Fern repeated helpfully, knowing that Kirsty would not ever call them by that 'indecent' name. She followed Brett outside.

'What got into you to shock poor old Kirsty?' Brett demanded as they walked towards the farm ute.

'She shouldn't have made me go with you, when I made it obvious that I didn't want to go,' Fern replied mutinously.

'But I wanted you to come,' Brett said as they drove off towards the back of the farm. 'After all, to quote Kirsty, "A man likes to get his girl to himself . . ." '

'Drop dead!'

Brett laughed cheerfully, 'I guess that would be one solution, but I'm not going to. I'm enjoying myself far too much.'

CHAPTER SEVEN

BRETT stopped the ute in the shade of the totara tree by the edge of the creek.

Fern got out and walked to the creek and looked in hopefully . . . Yes, there were three large brown trout in the deep pool, lazily waving their tails just enough to keep their place against the current. She had ridden up here quite often and had not been disappointed yet, there was always at least one trout in the pool at the bend of the creek, the sunlight shafting down through gaps in the trees sliced through the brownish creek water.

As Brett joined her, she asked, 'Where are the cattle you want me to help you with?'

'The cattle are over there, and I don't want to move them. I just want to talk to you, and settle a few points. Being engaged to you is very wearing, and a trifle more complicated than I anticipated.'

'*Charming!*' Fern said sarcastically. 'However, if you feel it too much of a strain after two hours, I'm more than willing to call the whole thing off.'

'There you go, biting my head off before I have a chance to explain . . . and you talk about me jumping to conclusions! I have no intention of breaking our engagement, but I thought if we sorted out a few of our differences, we could call a truce for a month or so, and we might even learn to enjoy each other's company.'

'No chance,' Fern said flatly.

Brett sat down and patted the grass beside him. 'Sit down, and take those damned dark glasses off. I find it difficult enough to guess what you're getting at, at the best of times, but with those glasses, it's impossible.'

Fern sat down a careful six feet away from him, adjusting her glasses more firmly, to show him she was not prepared to give an inch. After the way he had spoken to her in town this afternoon she thought she was being very magnanimous to even talk to him. 'If you've got anything else to criticize me for, I'd be pleased if you'd hurry up, because I want to get back and help Kirsty.'

'I wish you'd take a more reasonable attitude. You must have known that when we became engaged you'd have to be with me a lot more, not only with me, but close to me, and there you go sitting half a mile away. Uncle and Kirsty won't expect us to make wild passionate love whenever we're together, but they will at least expect that you would want to sit by me on the couch, that I should occasionally put my arm around you, or even hold your hand.'

'So . . .?'

Brett sighed, 'So I wish you wouldn't behave as if you'd discovered a python crawling around your neck whenever I put my arm across your shoulders, and if I take your hand, you react as if you'd been bitten by a deadly *katipo* spider, and when I kiss you . . .'

'Yes?' Fern watched him alertly.

'Surely to God you've been kissed before, there's no need to carry on like an outraged *prima donna*?'

Furious, Fern felt her cheeks burning. 'You know this is only a sham, there was no need to kiss me with such . . . Well, like you did in front of the Smiths.'

Brett laughed, 'What were you going to say? With such enthusiasm, or with such pleasure? You mean you wouldn't mind being kissed by me as long as I regarded it as a bore, but not if I actually enjoyed kissing you? Sorry, my angry witch-woman, I do enjoy kissing you . . .'

Fern broke in, 'Have you anything further to say, because I'm going home if I have to walk.' She stood up impatiently.

'Yes, I have. About the presents we'll be given, don't worry about them. Just keep a list, and if we don't stick together I'll return them to the donors, okay? The other thing is, I have to put an announcement in the papers.

Kirsty has already taken me to task for not doing it today. Have you any objections?'

'Yes. I'd rather you didn't, but if you have to, please not in one of the national papers, just the wee local paper that comes out twice a week. Oh, and I don't want my address, something along the lines of "Brett Alexander and Fern Fraser of Kowhiterangi have much pleasure in – blah-blah,' you know how it goes. I don't want my family to know anything about this.'

Brett stood up and stretched. 'Okay, don't you think they'd approve of me?'

'Oh, I'm sure they would think I was most fortunate to have caught someone as eminently suitable as you.'

Brett walked across and put his arms around her. 'But you don't consider yourself lucky?'

'No.'

'Fern, I wish you would try to be friends, it would make our association much more pleasant. If you would tell me what I do to annoy you, I'd stop it. What is it about me that you dislike so much?'

'Everything!' Fern said bitterly. Then before she could stop herself, she blurted out, 'If I'd known what you really thought of me I'd never have agreed to this engagement. You said I was hard and unforgiving, that there was nothing loving or feminine about me, that I was taking unfair advantage of your wish to please your uncle, by making you grovel, and that you'd be ashamed to introduce me to your friends, and now you have the flaming cheek to think I'd like to be friends with you! You can't complain, you were still willing to put a ring on my finger even after finding out what a bitch I am.' To her horror she was crying. 'You can go to hell! Sm-Smithy was so excited about us, she said you looked years younger, and that you l-l-loved me very much, s-she said she could tell by the way you never took your eyes off me.'

Fern found her handkerchief and blew her nose. 'I didn't disillusion the poor dear. You see, I knew why you were so happy, because you'd managed to please Uncle Hamish without being irrevocably tied to me. And you kept watching me because you were scared I would blow it. B-but I didn't, did I? It was you, when you found out Lisa was coming here after Christmas. You might have fooled them, but not me, you nearly broke my collarbone. I guess you just realized how stupid you were to grab me, when by waiting a few weeks you could have got the girl you really loved. Not to worry.' She took a deep breath. 'You can tell Lisa that this arrangement is pure fake, the day Uncle Hamish is buried I'll take off your ring, and disappear.'

Through her thin silk shirt she felt his hands on her back, drawing her closer to him, he held her, comforting her, soothing her as if she was a child. When she stopped crying he still held her, she could feel his cheek against her hair. 'Fern, I can't believe I said such terrible things to you. I must have been out of my mind. I can't even apologize . . . to say I'm sorry would be so trite after I'd hurt you so badly. I haven't any excuse to offer, except perhaps I was nervous about buying the ring . . . you see, I've never had any experience. Once before you were big enough to forgive me, do you think you could be that generous again, even though I don't deserve it?'

Fern nodded her head. As always after she'd quarrelled with someone she felt ashamed and drained of energy.

'Great. Now can we have a truce? I know we can get through the summer without too much friction, if we both try.'

Fern moved towards the ute. 'I'll buy that.'

Brett held the door open. 'Before you get in, I'll show you what I have in mind. It's called compromise. You know I don't like you wearing those dark glasses, and I know you don't like being kissed, so . . . we compromise. Every time I see you with those things on I'll take it as an invitation to kiss you. If you want to stop me just take them off. Starting from now.'

'From now? That's not fair.'

Brett cupped her face in his hands, and she felt his lips brush hers, once, twice, and then again. 'Now will you take them off?' he demanded. 'When I speak to you it's unnerving to get a beautiful reflection of the Southern Alps from where your eyes should be. It's like talking to a dead person whose soul has departed.'

Fern smiled. So the glasses were having the right effect, he could no longer read her thoughts. A kiss or two was a small price to pay for such privacy.

The next kiss was neither short, nor lightly taken. It left Fern shaken, and not a little angry that Brett should have the power to disturb her when she disliked him so much. She realized that she wasn't going to stand much more of this, but if she gave in now, all future compromises would be her giving and him taking. She saw the challenge in his blue eyes. Well, two could play at this game. When he kissed her again she would respond instead of standing there like a wooden Indian; that ought to scare the daylights out of him.

When his arms went around her, she moved into his embrace, and putting her arms around him, was delighted to feel his slight hesitation ... that was the last rational thought she had. As his lips met hers, seeking, searching, and demanding, she felt herself responding with a wild joyful passion over which she had no control, wishing that this experience would go on for ever. Then it was over, and she was conscious of his heart pounding in time with her own.

He gently guided her to the ute seat, and taking her glasses off he folded them and placed them in the pocket of her shirt. 'Enough is enough.'

He started the engine, but before letting the clutch out he turned towards her, and their eyes met for a long wordless moment. Fern was the first to look away. She took her glasses from her pocket and carefully and deliberately broke them in half.

'An excellent solution, Fern,' Brett said as he drove off.

Neither spoke on their way home. Fern was filled with

wonder and confusion as she tried to face the implications of the new situation in which she found herself involved. She had to admit, if only to herself, that she was physically attracted to Brett ... that was all, purely a physical thing. Also, because she wasn't a fool, she knew that Brett enjoyed holding her, and kissing her, in spite of the fact that he disliked almost everything about her: her behaviour, her way of dressing, and her opinion on practically everything under the sun. No wonder he was pleased with her for breaking the glasses; he had no intention of getting drawn into a difficult relationship with her when Lisa was due to arrive in a few weeks' time. Now that they were both aware of the danger, Fern was sure they would both be anxious not to aggravate it.

As they walked towards the house, Brett caught her arm. 'Then we can call a truce? After all, we are both civilized people.'

'I wouldn't count on it,' muttered Fern.

Brett laughed. 'I do. And remember, it's our business how we became engaged, and nobody else's. It's a pact between the two of us. I promise you that I won't speak of it to anyone. Can you give me your word too?'

'Certainly.' Fern knew he meant Lisa, and the fact that he could not say her name meant a lot. 'May I have my friendship ring back, please?'

'Sorry, but I don't think it good form to wear it when you've got my ring on.'

On entering the house, Fern found Kirsty in a mood that Smithy had described as 'sticky'. However, by asking her to help choose a suitable dress for that evening from among the new purchases, she got Kirsty to relent and follow her down the passage. She immediately touched the green full-length gown. 'This one, and if you would wear your hair up . . .?'

Fern nodded in agreement. 'I'll have my shower now, and change.'

As she took her seat beside Brett at the dinner table, Fern felt a little nervous. Was she capable of playing her part?

But these people were friends, and they were not looking for faults or flaws, being only too happy to rejoice with the newly engaged couple and show Fern how welcome she was to join the warm, close-knit group.

As she stood on the steps to say good night with Brett beside her, she knew that they had accepted her completely, and what had at first appeared to be an ordeal had in actual fact turned out to be a very pleasant evening.

Brett's finger flicked her cheek lightly. 'Thank you, Fern. Now, off to bed. You've had a busy day. Good night.'

By the time Fern had accompanied him to the house-warming the following Saturday night, she faced her own engagement party with much more assurance. Somehow it seemed no longer strange to be regarded as his fiancée. People took their engagement at face value, and Fern reacted accordingly, and became more relaxed. In her more mischievous moments, she even flirted a little with Brett as she became sure that he would not take advantage of it.

The engagement party was at its height when Brett forced his way through to Fern's side. He bent his head to whisper in her ear, 'You're wanted on the phone, a person-to-person call for you from Wellington.' He saw her eyes widen with fear. 'I've had it put through to my office; you wouldn't have a hope of hearing on the kitchen phone. Do you want me to go with you?'

Fern nodded mutely. Suddenly all the gaiety of the evening was gone. Something was wrong at home. They must have had police help to track her down, and her thoughts flew from her parents to her brothers and sister. They had promised not to try and contact her unless there was an emergency.

She sat in the office chair and reluctantly picked up the phone. 'Fern Fraser speaking.' After a few moments' delay, she heard her father's voice.

'That you, Fern?'

'Yes, Dad. What's wrong?'

'With us? Nothing at all. Your mother has been driving me

mad ever since she heard of your engagement this afternoon. She says, if *you* don't consider this an emergency, *she* does. She wants to know all about the young man.'

Bewildered, Fern asked, 'How did she find out?'

'Some school friend of yours down there wrote to her sister in Wellington enclosing a cutting of your engagement notice, and the girl mentioned it to someone else, and eventually it reached your mother. As she happens to be having one of her maternal moods, she threatened me with two options; that I rang you tonight or she would catch the plane to Hokitika tomorrow. You know that she doesn't normally worry about her offspring, bar taking a head count occasionally, but once she gets started on what she calls "her duty as a mother", nothing stands in her way.'

'I do not—'

'Hush, woman! You said I was to make the call and that's what I intend to do. As you can guess, Fern, your mother is on the extension—'

'Hi, darling,' Fern said, while her mind whirled busily, trying to think of how to stall her mother from carrying out her threat to fly to the Coast.

'Oh, Fern, I've been so *frantic*. Alison raved about how romantic it was, you having been knocked over by this madman and how he took you to his home and you're now going to marry him. She said you'd been unconscious in hospital and had lost your memory and were badly scarred. Is that true?'

'No.' Fern was feeling quite lightheaded with relief that everyone was well.

'What do you mean, no? Are you engaged to this . . . this idiot who ran you down? Why, you *can't* be. We don't even know his name.'

Fern's eyes flicked to where Brett was perched on the edge of the desk. 'Yes, I am engaged to him, he isn't an idiot, and his name is Brett Alexander. He didn't knock me down. His uncle was giving me a ride when we crashed, and I'm not scarred. Does that answer all your questions?'

'Not quite.' Her father had now taken control of the conversation. 'Why didn't you let us know? Are we going to have a chance to meet this young man who is not an idiot? When are you getting married?'

Fern ignored the first question, having no ready answer. 'Yes, of course you can meet him before we get married, and that won't be for simply ages.' She glanced up at Brett and received no help whatsoever. 'We're going to have a long engagement, a very long engagement.'

Mrs. Fraser again: 'Is he good-looking?'

Fern glared at Brett. 'Not at all good-looking. In fact, downright ugly.'

'Oh, I'm so pleased, Fern darling. Good-looking men are two a penny and have no character. Are you very much in love with him, baby?'

'No. I don't love him; I became engaged to him because I hated the very sight of him.'

'You're being facetious. Speak to her, Neil!'

'I will, if you would be kind enough to release the line for a moment. Well, Fern, why not let us in on such an important event in your life?'

Fern decided that the best defence lay in attack. 'You promised not to get in touch with me unless there was an emergency. I didn't consider this an emergency, so naturally I didn't inform you.'

'Not good enough. If you don't give us the real reason, I'll even drive your mother to the airport.'

Fern knew her father only too well. He didn't make empty threats. The thought of her mother coming threw Fern into a panic. Mrs. Fraser might act vague and not quite with it, but Fern had no doubt that if her mother made the scene, it would take her less than a day to turn up the facts. 'Hang on a moment, please, I've got to shut the door. I can't hear.'

Fern covered the mouthpiece with her hand. 'Brett, you've got to let me tell them it isn't real. I can't deceive them – not my parents.'

'You'll have to. For one thing, this is a party line, and you know what that means. For another, as it's taken only ten days for a garbled version to reach your mother, how long do you think it would take to travel back here?'

Fern had to admit he was right. She lifted the phone. 'You still there?'

'That must be a very large room you're in, considering the length of time it took you to shut the door,' her father remarked rather caustically.

'Sorry, I was trying to work out an answer that will satisfy you and not hurt anyone here,' Fern replied.

'Difficult?'

'More than somewhat.' Fern sighed. 'You see, Mr. Alexander is very ill indeed – that's Brett's uncle and his only relative. I'm sure you'd be both welcome to come, but I'd prefer it if you left it just now. They've got enough worries without having strangers in the house as well. I feel it would be unfair, and a further strain. Am I getting through to you?'

'The old chap needs you to nurse him, is that it? Am I correct in assuming that it will not be for long?'

'Yes!'

'Sorry to have pushed you so far. So I'll just offer you two my best wishes and trust that you'll bring Brett up to meet us. I wouldn't have rung but for your mother's imagination running riot. Good night, Fern, and God bless.'

'I want to know if I'd like him, Fern,' her mother demanded.

'Of course you would, darling. That's another idiotic question. You have very catholic tastes.'

'Yes, I suppose I have,' her mother said doubtfully, then, 'Hold on a minute, here's Duncan to congratulate you.'

'Hi, Mouse. Hear you've gone all clucky! I've only one question. Is he sexy?'

Fern laughed, because Duncan described everything from his car to his football boots as sexy. 'Oh, yes, very. Goodbye, everyone.' Duncan replaced the receiver and she heard a distinct click as she hung up. She gasped and then blushed as she caught Brett's eye. Someone had been listening in on the party line!

Brett's blue eyes were full of amusement. 'That must have been a very interesting conversation; the half I heard was quite intriguing. I hope your folks are pleased with their future son-in-law. You really gave them the hard sell. I'd love to know what they said at the end to bring such a glorious colour rushing to your cheeks.'

'You'll never know . . . well, not unless the person who was listening in tells you, and somehow I doubt if they will.'

Brett took her hand in his as she stood up. 'I'm glad it wasn't bad news, Fern. You were very frightened when you came in here. You're a bit of a fraud, aren't you? You pretend you don't care for your family, and they don't worry about you. Some day I'll want to learn a lot more about you, but just now I'm happy to be engaged to a very beautiful and charming young lady.'

Fern looked up, expecting to find him laughing at her, but he was suddenly serious. The quick retort which sprang to her mind was not spoken. She felt her eyes caught and held in his gaze and was aware of the tension building up between them. Conscious of his nearness and of the very real attraction between them, she waited, knowing that he was going to kiss her. When the door opened, letting a crowd of young people pour in, Fern was shocked at the anger and disappointment she felt. She was made sharply conscious of the tight rein that she would have to hold on her emotions. It was utter recklessness to become so engrossed in playing the part of Brett's fiancée that she began to believe that she was indeed intending to marry him.

Jane Hamilton and her partner led the group, and Jane said gaily, 'Come on, you two, break it up! You've got the rest of your lives together; tonight you're on display. Mr. Alexander sent us to fetch you. He wants to go to bed, but wants to make the formal announcement before he does.'

Brett and Fern followed the others back to the large

114

lounge, and when he took her hand in his as they stood beside Uncle Hamish, she felt again the curious heady sensation that had come over her in the office. Throughout the rest of the evening, she had a heightened awareness of Brett's presence, whether he was at her side, or moving among the guests with his pleasant easy manner. Somehow it was as if he too was conscious that they had entered another stage in their knowledge of each other.

Once as she watched him talking to an elderly couple across the room, he turned, as if feeling her gaze, and his eyes lit with laughter and yet managed to convey to her that he found her desirable, that he was proud to introduce her to his friends. She fought down the excitement she felt building up inside her. That was *dumb*. There was only going to be one person hurt if she played along with this, and that was Fern herself. She had to stop this new development dead cold. He was in love with Lisa, she had ample evidence of that. Of course he wasn't above a pleasant light-hearted affair with her to fill in time, but was Fern? She decided that the answer to that was a definite negative. She had to play it cool, real cool.

By the time the last guest had left, Fern had herself well in hand. It was her own fault for allowing Brett to believe that there could be anything more between them than ... say, respect, or perhaps friendship. From now on this engagement would remain on a strictly unemotional plane.

When they were alone at last Fern tried to convey the idea to Brett, with marked lack of success.

He was standing too close to her ... It was unnerving. 'Look at me, Fern.'

'No. I've made myself quite clear. You *do* know what a platonic friendship means, I hope?'

He laughed. 'Sure. No kissing, very dull. You surprise me, you really do. I could even say you disappoint me. I thought you were the sort to be honest if it killed you.'

That brought her head up fast. 'I am honest!'

'How honest?' he mocked her. 'In the office tonight you

knew I was going to kiss you?'

'Yes.'

'And you wanted me to?' he relentlessly pressured her.

Fern felt her cheeks burn. 'Yes.'

'And now you don't. What's changed?'

'I've had time to think.'

'And you think you wouldn't enjoy being kissed by me?' His finger delicately traced the outline of her face.

Fern held his gaze with difficulty. She knew that she wanted to be kissed by him, more than she'd ever wanted anything before. She knew she only had to lean towards him a fraction of an inch and she would be in his arms. She was trembling, but she stood her ground. 'I didn't say that. What I said was that I didn't want you to kiss me, not now, not ever. We might have weeks or months to live with this engagement and I think it's better for both of us if we keep it cool.'

'Sounds more like a deep freeze.' His eyes searched her face and noted the brilliance of unshed tears in her brown eyes, and the defiant tilt of her small chin.

To her immense relief, he walked over to the fireplace and lit a cigarette. It was only then that she discovered she had been holding her breath.

'Okay, Fern, I'll let you call the shots, for now.' He watched the smoke curl up from his cigarette. 'Beats me why your mother called you Fern ... Rose would have been much more appropriate.'

'Why?' Fern asked, surprised at the turn of the conversation.

'Well, like a rose, you look good, you smell good, but if someone takes hold of you they end up picking out the thorns.'

'I'm sorry,' and she meant it. After all, she had led him on a bit.

'Don't be sorry. We've come a long way in a short time. We started out by despising each other, and now you want to make like we're Hansel and Gretel. That's progress, if you like!'

'Hansel and Gretel were brother and sister,' Fern pointed out.

Brett smiled at her. 'Got it in one. You are quick. Impossible, isn't it – or do you feel sisterly towards me?'

'I'm going to bed. Good night.'

For a week or so after the party, Fern kept a wary eye on Brett, but he gave her no cause for alarm. When they were alone he treated her with the almost casual indifference of an older brother, and in the presence of others he gave a good impression of a happily engaged man without overdoing it. At first she felt very pleased, but as the days passed she was a little piqued that he should have taken her suggestion so literally. She was sorely tempted to try and provoke some response from him, but resisted ... she wasn't that sure of him or of herself.

The lovely long golden days of summer slipped past, and the work on the farm speeded up. Fern found herself becoming more and more involved in the running of the farm. She was interested in every new experience. Mr. Alexander had good days, and others when he was content to stay in bed. He flatly refused to allow Fern to spend too much time with him. 'You get out on the farm, Fern. You be my eyes now that I can't get around so well.'

Between milkings Ross and Robbie spent most of their time on the tractors, topdressing with fertilizers, and planting swedes for the winter. They were always glad of a spare hand to take a broken piece of machinery into town for repairs, or to bring the cows in, and Brett called on her often to help with mustering the sheep for shearing or drafting off the fat lambs. She could ride much better now, and while she preferred the cattle work, she knew the dairy herd must be watched with a vigilant eye to detect first signs of bloat, which could wipe out a whole herd if they broke through an electric fence and consumed more than their share of the rich clover.

Animals had to be drenched for parasites, sprayed for lice, and all the dairy land boom-sprayed to keep the ragwort under control. Of course Fern wasn't out with the men all the time. Kirsty had first call on her time. The best part of the day was when the work was finished, and she went with Brett and Robbie and Maureen down to the river to swim. It meant a short walk across the paddock from the house and then a drop down to a grass bank below the willows where the river ran smooth and deep. Sometimes Jane Hamilton and her cousins would join them, but more often than not it was just the four of them. Refreshed from their swim, they would relax on the bank, sometimes in companionable silence, but mostly discussing or arguing about a subject that interested them. Occasionally Fern would catch Brett watching her with a curious speculative expression and she would suddenly realize that she was giving her own views and not the outrageous radical opinions of her brothers. She would be annoyed at showing him more of herself than she had meant to, and so would jump to her feet and pick up her towelling wrap, calling, 'Who's for home?' As they paired off to walk home in the gathering dusk she would console herself that it was a two-way exchange; now she no longer felt it necessary to challenge his every statement it gave her time to know him and have a reluctant respect for his quick wit and rare perception.

Coming in the middle of the busy farm season, Christmas passed with scarcely a ripple. When Fern opened one of her presents and found a pair of dark glasses, she had no need to look at the note to see who had given them.

'Aren't you going to try them on to see if they fit?' Brett asked with seeming innocence.

Fern felt her face grow warm. 'No. They're very nice, but I think I'll save them for a rainy day.'

It really didn't help when Kirsty looked surprised and said, 'Oh, I thought today would be the very day to wear them, it's so sunny.'

Mr. Alexander was in particularly good health and stayed

up all day. In the evening he asked Kirsty to bring him several photograph albums, and as he turned page after page of the faded photographs Fern found a new and deeper understanding of the farm and what it meant to the old man. It was difficult to believe that the smooth green paddocks she knew today had been a large dreary expanse of cutover bush left behind when the trees had been milled originally, and gorse and blackberry everywhere. It must have taken a lot of imagination, determination and hard work to bring it to its present perfection. No wonder Mr. Alexander felt that he was part of the farm and it was part of him; it was his whole life's work.

The next album started with a wedding photograph of Brett's parents. Fern scanned the later snapshots, trying to see what had made Mr. Alexander compare her with Brett's mother, but she looked in vain. There was no resemblance. Brett's mother had been very beautiful, dainty, almost fragile, yet there was real character in her face. There were many photographs of her, mostly laughing, sometimes standing on top of a drayload of hay, or riding with her husband, or at a picnic. There was no doubting that she was very happy in her marriage. Brett was the image of his father, a tall dark sinewy man, and many photos of Kirsty and her husband, a younger softer Kirsty, as bridesmaid at her cousin's wedding, and later sharing work and pleasure with the Alexanders, told Fern how close the families must have been.

Then came the shots of Donald Alexander in a rough, ill-fitting khaki uniform, and one of him and his wife standing beside Kirsty and her husband on their final leave. What had Kirsty said? 'Donald came back; my husband didn't come home.' Fern wished she could ask Mr Alexander not to go on, but the lump in her throat prevented her from speaking. If these people could have survived the cruel blows and come through not crippled in spirit, but somehow made stronger, it was a small thing for her to relive the past through these photographs.

The next series was of Donald coming home, taller, thinner, and with the strain on his face telling of what he had been through more than any words could have. Then scores of snaps of Brett as a baby, and more of the men working on the house, and Brett in each photo. Then another page turned, and without warning she was looking at the headstone erected over the young couple.

Without showing any emotion, Mr. Alexander picked up the last album. These were all of Brett . . . Brett's first day at school, catching his first fish, shooting his first deer, with his football team. Then each page from then on was conspicuous with missing photographs. Fern knew enough of the family history to realize that someone must have gone through systematically removing every snap of Brett and Lisa. She wondered who had done it – Kirsty or Uncle Hamish before Brett came back from the U.S.A., or perhaps Brett had removed them after his return. She would never know, but in a way their absence made Lisa more important than she would have been if those blank spaces had not jumped out at her. The rest of the photographs were of Brett's tour through Britain, Canada, and the U.S.A. The last one was of the day Brett arrived back. He was standing between Kirsty and his uncle. Had nothing happened since then, to be considered worth recording?

At least she had learned something. She had often thought it a pity that Kirsty and Uncle Hamish had not married; now she knew why they had not. Kirsty would never have entertained the thought of marrying again, and even if she had it would have been no use. From the wedding photograph of Grace and Donald right through the album, Fern had gained the impression that both the Alexander brothers had loved the same woman. Life had been very unfair to Hamish, Fern reflected. Then as she watched Brett helping his uncle to his bed, she knew she was all wrong. The farm and having the care and charge of Brett since he was a baby had filled Hamish's life completely.

She stood and stretched. 'I'll make supper now, Kirsty.'

Kirsty nodded. 'Good idea. I don't want any; I'll be away to my bed. You can make coffee for yourself and Brett.'

She helped Kirsty tidy up the lounge, then went through to make the coffee and cut two generous slices of rich dark Christmas cake.

Brett joined her as she poured the coffee. 'Sorry I was so long. Uncle was a bit wound up tonight. Here, he asked me to give you this. It belonged to his mother.'

Fern held the heavy pendant in her hand. It was a Celtic cross with highly polished stones set in silver, the four brilliant coloured stones set with narrow bases about a tiny silver chased cross, blue and green and gleaming zebra-stripe, and at the base a long misty stone descending through pearl and yellow to a clear red-orange. The stones were framed in clear silver and an engraved silver halo linked them about the centre.

She put it back on the table beside Brett. 'I can't accept this. He thought he was giving it to your future wife.' She took up her coffee mug and cupped her hands around it, feeling grateful for the warmth even though the night was warm and mild.

'He might have been,' Brett answered with a smile. Then seeing she seriously intended to refuse, he went on, 'What an independent child you are! Take it. Uncle Hamish had the same thought as you, except he put it in a different way. He said there was often a slip 'twixt cup and lip, and whether or no, you were to have this pendant.'

'Then he doesn't believe we're really engaged. All this has been for nothing,' Fern interrupted.

'He hasn't guessed a thing. He said that if I didn't get you to the altar, it would be my own damned fault, that I was being stupid, that I wasn't showing you enough affection, and finally that every girl liked to be told quite often how much she was loved. Sterling advice. Fern, would you like me to tell you how much I love you – I mean, at decently spaced intervals?'

Fern coloured under her smooth apricot tan. 'I love

Uncle, I think he's a marvellous person, and I think you're dead rotten to make fun of him.'

She finished her coffee, and took Brett's mug. 'Hurry and eat that other piece of cake so that I can wash the plate. I put two bits out for you.'

'You'd rather I took his advice seriously?' Brett queried, and Fern could hear the amusement in his voice.

'*Drop dead!*'

'What a fierce wee thing! You are a strange girl.'

'You've said that before,' Fern said angrily.

'I know. It's just that one moment you're so soft and vulnerable, like when you were going through those photos tonight. You were actually living through the troubles this family has had, and when you saw my parents' memorial stone you were nearly sick as if it was something obscene.'

'To me it was. He had been giving all his life and just when he had time for some living and loving to enjoy – his wife, his son, a new farm, and building a new house . . .' She stopped, unable to go on.

'You feel things too deeply, Fern. I haven't missed my parents, I had Kirsty and Uncle Hamish. I was too young to remember my mother and father. You were the only one torn apart this evening. Kirsty and Uncle weren't upset, because they'd lived through it all a long time ago. You saw it all in an hour and felt it all happened at once.'

He walked over and put the plate on the sink beside her. 'See what I mean? – sometimes sensitive and sympathetic, and another time as hard as nails. When I bared my soul pleading for love, you offered me Christmas cake. You really know how to hurt a guy. Do you know that my father wasn't much older than me when he died and he'd really done some living, not merely existing, not to mention loving. In his short married life I bet he received more love than many men get if they live to be a hundred. So get your priorities right.'

When Fern did not answer, he lifted the long curtain of

her hair aside and kissed her cheek gently. 'How someone as soft as you survived three years' nursing is a ruddy miracle.'

'Who told you I was a nurse?'

'Your friend Jane Hamilton.'

'With a friend like her who needs enemies?' snapped Fern.

'There you go! Ruffle your fur a little and you come out fighting. I'm going out to enjoy the moon and the stars, it's a beautiful night. When you've finished drying the pattern off those coffee mugs you can join me if you want to, but I really won't expect you.'

As he went out, Fern thought savagely that he was in for a big surprise. When he had kissed her, she felt her bones turn to water. It was then that she knew that she'd been what Robbie would call 'a steaming great twit'. Admittedly their engagement had got off to a pretty shaky start, but if she'd been a little bit loving towards him instead of this brother and sister bit, who knows what might have happened. Perhaps she'd been building Lisa up too big ... well, Lisa wasn't coming till next week, so tonight was hers. She put the dishes away and dried her hands, then went out, closing the door behind her. Brett was right, it *was* a beautiful night, the moon was on the wane but lost nothing from that, the deep velvet of the night sky was pin-cushioned with stars. Then she became conscious of Brett whistling a lilting melody and walked towards the sounds.

She stood in front of him. 'What's the name of that tune?'

She melted into his arms as he said, 'Don't look now, but your ignorance is showing. That was from Robbie Burns. I cut my teeth on Robbie Burns.'

He sang softly,

> 'Gin a body meet a body
> Coming through the rye;
> Gin a body kiss a body,
> Need a body cry?'

'I won't cry.'

'Ah, Fern . . .' and he drew her closer to him.

Some time later Fern heard the lounge clock chime twelve. 'Brett, it's midnight. We'd better go in.'

'Why? Do I get left with a glass slipper in my hand while you drag off in a pumpkin coach?'

'No.'

'Good. I guess you're still thinking you're back at the nurses' home and have to be in by twelve. Don't worry, I'll give you a late pass.' He kissed her again. 'Abstinence truly does make the heart grow fonder.'

'That's absence, not abstinence,' Fern corrected.

'The difference is too subtle for me . . . I like it best my way. Why did you come out tonight? It's not a very Gretel thing to do.'

'I was scared . . . not of you but of the moonlight. This valley is glorious during the day, but when the moon comes out it has a special magic.'

'So if you were scared why come?'

'Well, it's Christmas night. What better night for a little enchantment?'

'Fern darling. I think I've done a very stupid thing. I think I've fallen in love with you. Do you believe you could come to care for me? We could make this engagement real, very real.'

Fern was silent for a long time. She knew that it would take so little, a nod of her head, a simple 'yes' and he would respond immediately and so set the seal on their engagement and marriage. And she did *want* that so very much. But it wasn't right to snatch and grab at happiness, she had to be sure. Knowing Brett's character so well by now, she was sure that he would never ask for his ring back, not even if he found it was Lisa he had always wanted. She couldn't risk that; she would wait until she saw how he reacted to Lisa.

At last she said, 'I don't know. I'm sorry, Brett, but I would have to be very sure . . .'

'And I would want you to be very sure. Are you scared

that your answer may be influenced by the moonlight? Do you want to study my suggestion in the cold light of day?'

'Something like that,' Fern agreed.

'Well, I thought I'd get a resounding "No", so I'm very pleased with your answer. We're really making progress.'

Much later when Fern went to bed, she lay awake wondering if she'd been a fool not to take the chance. She loved him. She wanted him. She had not intended him to react so quickly, she had only been trying to shorten the odds when he made his final decision. And she slept.

CHAPTER EIGHT

THE sun was well up when Fern woke next morning. As she groped for her watch on the dressing table she felt anew that wild heady sensation of admitting to herself that she was in love with Brett. The thought of facing him this morning was exciting . . . would he go back to the Hansel and Gretel bit? She doubted that . . . not after last night. And she didn't want him to, because she only had a few days left before Lisa came. At least it wouldn't be a complete walkover by Lisa, not if Fern had her way. When she finally glanced at her watch she saw it was nearly nine o'clock. She launched herself out of bed and ran through to the shower.

Back in the bedroom she quickly dressed in minute shorts with her yellow shirt, and, because she was feeling young and happy, she plaited her hair in neat schoolgirl braids.

She hurried out to the kitchen. 'Good morning, Kirsty, and a fine large morning it is!' She had copied this form of greeting from one of the neighbours, and found it fitted her mood particularly well today.

'You're very late up this morning.' Kirsty almost sounded severe.

'Sorry,' Fern apologized. 'If you needed me to help, you should have called me.'

Kirsty still looked grim. 'I'm thinking it's the early bird that catches the worm. Have a look out the window.'

Fern walked across and looked out towards Smith's, and swiftly the morning gladness left her as she fixed her eyes on Brett with his arm around a gorgeous blonde. As she watched the girl put her hands up and pulled him down to kiss her.

'You're dead right, Kirsty, that's a rare bird out there, and boy, is he a *worm*?' She didn't even attempt to hide the bitterness in her voice.

126

'There now, girl, don't be after blaming Brett. I'm thinking he won't be pleased with her making such a spectacle of him.'

'He's feeling no pain.'

Kirsty looked at her sharply. 'And you, Fern? Do you feel no pain either?'

Fern turned away, knowing that Kirsty had clearly seen the hurt in her eyes. 'I'll make myself a cup of tea and a slice of toast. I don't feel very hungry.' She filled the electric jug and plugged it in, and put the toast in the toaster. She knew Kirsty was waiting for an answer to her question. Fern waited till she had on her 'professional face.' A nurse soon learned that no matter what was happening in her personal life she must preserve her untroubled face on duty, calm, serene, and confident.

She poured herself a cup of tea, then smiled at Kirsty. 'I wouldn't be honest if I said no. But what sort of a friend would I be to Brett if I stood in his way now that Lisa's come? To me it's quite obvious he does love her.'

'You'll be no friend of his if you let yon girl have him.' Kirsty became more Scottish under stress.

'What have you got against her? I thought everyone loved her?' Fern went on buttering her toast, without showing any emotion.

Kirsty spluttered, 'I – I'm thinking you would have got your information from a man. Lisa never wasted her talent on women. She all but ruined that boy's life, and you sit there eating toast, when you should be out putting that young madam in her place.'

Fern waved her piece of toast casually. 'What do you expect me to do? Rush out and hang one on her? Sorry. I don't believe in fighting over a man. There's an old saying, "Never run after a man or a bus. There'll be another one along shortly." Even if I wanted to interfere there's nothing I can do. Brett is no longer a boy, he's a man . . . he'll make his own decision. Don't you trust him?'

Kirsty answered angrily, 'I would not trust any man with

that one. She's cold and calculating, and selfish to the marrow bone, but she kens fine how to charm a man. Why, if you would go out there and speak to Brett, your presence might bring him to his senses.'

Fern said with a smile, 'Oh, I was just thinking of having a few words with him. I want something from my room, then I'll join them.'

Kirsty's worried face relaxed. 'You're a good girl, Fern. I knew I could rely on you.'

As Fern went to her room, she knew that Kirsty would never forgive her for what she was going to do. She picked up the dark glasses, still in their cellophane wrapping . . . he could have these back with his rotten ring. Under her apparently calm composure she was shocked to know just how much she cared, shocked also to feel the seething, burning pangs of jealousy – a hitherto unknown experience.

Mr. Alexander called her to take his tray out. Fern thanked him for the pendant, but he brushed her thanks aside. 'It was a small thing to give you when you've given me so much. I don't mean the hours you've spent with me, wasting your time listening to an old man blethering away, although I am grateful for that too. No, it's much more than that, you've given me peace of mind. When the time comes, I'll slip away easily knowing that Brett's future is with you, that his children and yours will grow up here at Matai Valley. The Lord has been good to me, but he saved the best gift for last. Brett has grown hard and cynical these last years, he's forgotten what it is to enjoy life to the full. Then you came in, wild, free, honest and independent. It pleased me to see you stand up to him and knock holes in that armour-plating of his, and yet with all your strength you haven't lost any of the qualities a man wants in a wife – a warm, loving, generous heart, and the ability to laugh in the face of adversity. Brett is a very fortunate young man and I am content.'

A hard lump in Fern's throat prevented her from speaking, so she bent down and kissed his old wrinkled cheek.

He caught her hand as she stood up. 'You do love him, Fern? You wouldn't lie to me?'

'No, I wouldn't lie to you, Uncle Hamish. I love Brett. Now can I straighten up your bed?'

'No, you cannot. I'm going back to sleep, and I don't want you messing about with my bed when I've just got it comfortable. Away with you!'

At the back door she met Robbie with the milk billy. 'Hi, Fern. Did you get a load of that?' He jerked his hand in the direction of Smith's. 'Put this on the bench, then I'll take you over to the "I love Lisa" group.'

Fern did as she was told, then walked slowly beside Robbie. 'Do you know her? When did she arrive?'

'She arrived last night. I thought you would have heard the commotion.'

Fern did not reply. She was thinking that last night she had been in a world of her own, just Brett and herself.

Robbie carried on, 'Well, Smithy was a bit put out, really. Lisa wasn't supposed to come till next week, then she rang last night from town to say she couldn't get accommodation, and could she come out. Smithy had to say "yes", but she was fair sizzling. Anyone who knows the Coast knows that the place is fully booked months before Christmas. It wasn't till Lisa threw herself on Ross, and covered him with kisses, that Smithy lost her cool ... Hey, stop!' Fern stood still, while Robbie walked around her. 'Yeah, you'll do.'

'*Charming!*'

'Don't get off your bike. I was going to suggest that you go and get into that new gear you've got, but weight for age you should win hands down.'

'I'm not a racehorse!' Fern replied cuttingly, although her heart warmed towards Robbie.

'Belt up! You know what I mean. You in that shirt thing and plaits, no shoes, you look about fifteen. All that's missing is the braces on your teeth. She's mutton dressed as lamb, but you're the real thing.'

'If you think I'm a lamb, you're in for a shock.' She sang

in a gravelly voice, 'He was her man, but he done her wrong.'

'Great man, you're out of sight. I knew you wouldn't chicken out of a fight. So did Smithy.'

Fern thought it was rather nice of Kirsty, Robbie and Smithy to be favouring her, but what they didn't know was that she had no right to hold Brett. There they were waiting for her to do something dramatic, and all she could think of was to heave his ring back with a few well-chosen words. She knew what Mr. Alexander's reaction would be ... it was no use upsetting him at this stage. W-e-l-l, she might just wait a little, to see which way the cookie crumbled.

'If you don't move you'll grow roots,' Robbie broke into her thoughts rudely.

Fern went forward, her temper somehow cooling, but there was no ease of the pain which grabbed her when she saw that Brett was holding hands with Lisa on one side, and a tiny fair girl of about six on the other.

'Hi, everyone.' Fern was pleased that she managed to get the greeting out with commendable nonchalance.

Ross, with a smile, said, 'Catching up on your beauty sleep, Fern?'

Fern, in the mood to take any remark as personal, felt she was being compared with Lisa's fresh blonde prettiness, and compared unfavourably at that. And who could blame him? Lisa need not shrink from a close scrutiny. She was small and curvy, with a glorious peaches-and-cream complexion, baby blue eyes, and her hair, worn short, had been styled by an expert. Huh! A chocolate-box beauty! Fern thought scornfully ... and then more honestly ... who the heck was she to knock such loveliness when she, at this moment, would trade her two extra inches, and smooth tan if she could swop them for a tenth of Lisa's man-appeal.

'Glad you came over, Fern.' Brett's welcome was warm. 'Meet an old friend of mine, Lisa Tremaine, and her children, Sally and Simon.'

Before Fern could reply, Lisa laughed merrily, 'No, I

don't believe it! A child bride! I thought there was a law against that in New Zealand. Why, you great big cradle-snatcher, you!'

'Cradle-snatching is what I do best,' Brett replied with a laugh.

'Good morning, Mrs. Tremaine . . .'

This sent Lisa into fresh spasms of laughter. 'Please don't, I can't bear it. Call me Lisa.'

Fern's eyes darkened. 'I was taught to be polite to older women.'

For a moment Lisa's mask dropped, and she gave Fern a look of pure dislike, then she looked up at Brett. 'Ouch! that child bride of yours can scratch. Tell her, Brett baby, that she's to be nice to little Lisa.'

'I should have warned you, Lisa. Fern may be young, but she can sure defend herself. If you ask her nicely, I'm sure she'll oblige.'

Fern felt sick as she saw Lisa rub her face against Brett's arm. Why, she was almost purring! So that was what Robbie meant, not acting like a lamb, but kittenish behaviour. Brett baby! Yuk! And what was he looking so smug about? Fern realized that Lisa had won that point ... insulting her wasn't the way to beat her. And Fern had no intention of letting Brett enjoy the pleasure of being fought over.

Lisa giggled, and twirled around, still holding Brett's hand. She was now in the circle of his arm. 'Fern, please? Pretty please? Not Mrs. Tremaine, but Lisa. Oh, don't you think my children are adorable? Brett does. Don't you, Brett baby? Sally, go and kiss Fern.'

Like a well-trained puppet the wee girl obediently presented herself, and Fern, not wanting to upset her, bent and kissed her, but she would have preferred to get to know Sally first, and then be kissed if the child liked her.

'Now Simon, you kiss Fern as well.'

'Me Jack.'

'Simon,' Lisa's voice sharpened, 'do as you're told!'

Simon stood up, a sturdily built boy of three. 'Me Jack.'

There was defiance in his voice, and even his posture, his small fat legs spread well apart, and his head up. 'Me Jack.'

Lisa managed to smile, but Fern knew she was furious. 'Isn't it absolutely maddening? We had a crazy old chap in mowing the lawn, and his name was Jack. Simon adored him, even to the extent of taking his name. But I will not have it. For the last time, Simon, go and kiss Fern or Mummy will smack you.'

Simon neither moved nor spoke. Lisa went to him and shook him angrily, then slapped him hard on his bare legs. 'Do as I say!'

Fern was shocked. The cute little mother with two adorable children act had been blown to bits. Poor little fellow, he had the marks of Lisa's hand standing out red on his legs. Fern was beside him in an instant. She knelt down. 'Hello, Jack. Will you shake hands with me? I don't like being kissed, and I'd like to be friends with you.'

Simon regarded her steadily, then wiping the tears from his blue eyes, he put out his hand. 'Me Jack.'

'Me Fern.' She shook his hand solemnly. 'Would you like to come and see Gypsy, my horse?'

Simon nodded his head, and Fern swept him into her arms, out of Lisa's reach. 'Coming, Robbie? Would you like to come, Sally?'

Sally glanced quickly at her mother, then, 'No, thank you. It was kind of you to ask me.'

Fern didn't know which child she felt more sorry for, Simon, with his dark hair and stubborn chin, fighting to become an individual, or Sally, like a small golden fairy, already completely submissive.

Robbie walked beside her. 'Bitch, vicious bitch!'

Fern shook her head at him warningly. 'Not in front of the kid, that won't help him.'

'Fern!' Lisa had followed them, her voice came like a pistol shot. 'How dare you interfere when I'm disciplining Simon? You're actively encouraging him to defy me. I tell you, it's very difficult to be a solo parent . . .'

'Yes, I'm sure it is,' Fern agreed quickly, trying to pacify Lisa in case Simon was in for some more discipline. 'I was only trying to help by giving him something else to think about. Please let me take him to see Gypsy, then I'll bring him back to Smith's.'

'Put him down! There's only one way to deal with Simon. "Spare the rod and spoil the child" is one thing I'm not going to do. The little brat only responds to a good hard smack.'

'You can go off some people,' Robbie remarked to no one in particular.

Lisa's eyes were ice-blue. 'Young man, you're being impertinent! I'll speak to Brett about you. I wouldn't be at all surprised if you were dismissed.'

'Here's Brett baby coming now. Go to it! But remember that he doesn't enjoy seeing kids flattened any more than I do.' Robbie was completely unrepentant.

'Thought I'd join the party, because Sally has changed her mind, and decided to look at Gypsy too. Here, give me that boy, Fern. You're starting to get bandy legs, hefting a weight like Simon.'

'Me Jack,' and Simon nestled closer to Fern.

'How about that, Lisa? I'm not going to get to know your son while I continue to call him Simon. It's probably a silly phase he's going through, and if we all call him Jack, ten to one he'll run round saying "Me Simon". Shall we try it for a few days?'

'Do you think it would work like that? Honestly, he's been driving me up the wall!'

For an answer Brett took Simon from Fern with a cheerful, 'Come on, Jack, ' and Fern thought he was darned smart to have got them all out of a bad spot.

Lisa's smile was sweet and wistful. 'Thank you, Brett. It's just wonderful to have a man's advice. Sally was so easy to manage when she was little, but Simon has been a devil of a kid from the day he could walk – of course he takes after his father. Ted was stubborn and aggressive, too.'

Robbie whispered to Fern, 'He must have been quite a guy. I wish I'd met him.'

Lisa looked over towards them. 'If you two have anything else you'd rather do, Brett will give the children a ride.'

Brett replied, 'Don't worry, Lisa, it's a holiday today. Boxing Day. Fern and I are going in to the Boxing Day sports in Hokitika after lunch.'

'Can I go too?' Lisa pleaded. 'I remember now, all the chopping competitions and Highland dancing, running races, and kids looking for a needle in a haystack. It was fun. I'll ask Smith if she'll look after Sally and Simon.'

'Smithy is going to the sports,' Robbie said with a grin.

Fern startled them all by saying, 'I'll stay home and look after the children for you, Lisa. I was going to spend the afternoon down by the river swimming and sunbathing, so they'll be no trouble.'

'Thank you, Fern, that's good of you.'

Brett had a puzzled expression on his face. 'Sure you don't want to come, Fern?'

'Quite sure. I had a very late night last night, and am too lazy to go far from home. If I take care of the kids you and Lisa can stay as late as you like.'

'We'll take the kids with us,' Brett said flatly.

Fern gave them a pleasant smile, tossed her plaits over her shoulder and said, 'Suit yourselves, the offer is still open if you change your minds.'

Robbie caught up with her as they sauntered towards the house. 'What the hell do you think you're doing? Brett really wanted you to go to the sports with him. And what do you do but shove them together, then to top it off offer to look after the kids . . . Boy, are you dumb?'

'Thanks for the vote of confidence.' Fern was quite unperturbed. 'Did you think she was coming on a bit strong?'

'Did I *ever*! She'll eat him alive, he won't have a chance.

If I called you a half-wit I'd be paying you a compliment.'

Fern looked down her nose. 'Young man, you are being impertinent, I'll speak to Brett.' She laughed at Robbie's angry young face. 'Hey, man! Stay loose. I'm in full control of my faculties.'

'You mean you have a plan?' Robbie questioned doubtfully.

'Well, I wouldn't call it anything so grand as a plan. It's more or less an idea. Just remember, if you want me to carry your money in the matrimonial stakes, I'll do it my way or not at all. At the moment I don't think he's worth fighting for. I think he deserves her. Why have you got such a thing about her? I've never known you to be so rude to anyone. She's quite dishy really.'

'Yeah, the packaging is okay, but the product inside is inferior. Talk about selfish ... she was going on to Smithy last night how mean her mother was, you'd never believe it. When her husband divorced Lisa, he gave her a real generous settlement, but she got so bored staying at home with the kids that she took a job. Nothing wrong with that, of course. But she dumped the kids on her mother, who isn't strong, according to Smithy. Well, Lisa was angry when her mother's doctor ordered her to take a month's complete rest away from the kids. Is Lisa concerned about her mother? Is she heck! No, her mother let her down badly by getting sick when Lisa was due for her holidays. It sticks out a mile that she came haring over here to let Smithy take her mother's place, while she gets Brett lined up for the altar. Smithy is too canny to be caught like that, but you played right into Lisa's hands this morning.'

'Poor Lisa, so that's why she's so hopeless with those kids. She really doesn't know how to handle them, especially Me Jack, the darling. I suppose she's been out at work since he was a baby.'

Robbie muttered something under his breath, then, 'If you're going to feel sorry for her, I'm leaving you to it.

Keep in mind the fact that there was no need for her to go to work, so if her own kids are strangers to her, that's her own fault . . . See you.'

Fern checked with Kirsty, but was told there was nothing to do as lunch was cold meat, lettuce, and tomatoes.

Fern went to her room, and picked up her bikini and towelling beach wrap. She stopped in the kitchen to make a cut lunch to take with her, and when Kirsty commented that it wasn't enough to keep a bird alive, Fern answered, 'I'm not very hungry, Kirsty. Brett is taking Lisa and the kids down to the sports, so I thought I'd spend the afternoon by the river. Okay by you?'

Kirsty frowned, 'I'm thinking you are running away?'

Fern gave her what she hoped was a cheerful smile, and gathering up her things, said, 'I'm thinking you could be right.'

She went outside quickly before Kirsty could reply. Coming back from Gypsy's paddock was Brett with 'Me Jack' riding high on his shoulders, his free hand holding Sally's hand, and Lisa walking slightly in front of the group. As Fern watched, she saw Lisa turn and say something, and they were all laughing. It was like a TV commercial shot of a happy loving family, the big dark man and the sturdy boy, a dainty wife and her fair daughter.

The picture stayed with Fern as she crossed the road, then sprinted for the willows, and was still there as she changed and dived cleanly into the cool depths of the green river. She surfaced facing what Robbie called a baby Niagara, and made up her mind to try it. Robbie and Brett had swum up the white waters several times, and had laughed at Fern and Maureen's feeble attempts to fight their way through the swirling currents to the calm water above.

The river flowed around a bend, and finding itself pushed away from the bank by fallen trees and debris left by floods, foamed angrily through a narrow gap. Fern had tried it, but had always been swept back into the swimming pool, but today she was determined. She swam with strong, even strokes, aiming towards the outer edge of the whirling water, and soon felt her body caught in the fierce current, but this time fought against the pull of it even though she felt she was swimming hard just to keep her place. Tired and nearing the end of her strength, she battled on, then was suddenly caught in a cross-current and thrown through the gap and out into the smooth deep water on the other side. Completely exhausted in mind and body, she dragged herself on to the bank and lay down, feeling she had won a tremendous victory.

She dried off quickly in the hot sun, but lay there refreshed and relaxed, making no move to return downstream to her belongings. A shadow moved over her, shutting out the sun, and she turned to see if the sun had gone behind a cloud. She found Brett staring down at her.

'What the hell are you up to? Were you trying to drown yourself? You know that's a dangerous part of the river. You could have been sucked under and caught in the roots of those trees.'

Fern, feeling oddly lightheaded, giggled, 'If that was my intention, I've failed miserably.'

Brett bent down and caught her hands and pulled her not too gently to her feet. Had he always been that tall? And were his eyes always such a deep blue?

She didn't have much time for detached speculation, because Brett was kissing her as she'd never been kissed before. She felt weak with love for him, yet in the midst of the sweetness of his kiss, the memory came slicing through her of the disappointment and bitterness of seeing him kissing Lisa this morning.

She jerked free of his arms. 'Keep your kisses for Lisa, she might enjoy them – I don't!' She marched angrily along the beaten track beneath the willows.

Brett followed and waited until she had picked up her wrap and drawn it around her. 'You're a liar, Fern Fraser, if you say you didn't enjoy that kiss.'

'Then I'm a liar . . . who cares? Who do you think you

are? Alexander the Great? This morning I intended to hand your ring back, but I can't even do that, because Uncle Hamish laid it on me . . . he could die happy, knowing that you and I were going to be married. So there you have it — unless you want to hurt him badly, you're stuck with me, and I'm stuck with you while he's alive. I don't think it will be long, so you can consider yourself free to make any arrangements you like for afterwards, but in the meantime I expect you to keep up your side of the bargain, and I'll keep wearing your ring.'

Brett's expression was unreadable. 'So it *was* only moon-magic last night, Fern?'

Fern would not meet his eyes, so looked away and shrugged her shoulders. He could make what he liked of that gesture. She only wished he would go away and leave her alone.

He tried again. 'Kirsty seemed to think you were upset by Lisa's arrival. Is that true?'

Fern was fighting her instinct to lash out at him and hurt him as she had been hurt, but she knew that if she was going to carry on here she had to pretend indifference. 'Kirsty was upset. Perhaps you misunderstood her.'

Brett watched her thoughtfully. 'No, I don't think I misunderstood her. What do you think of Lisa?'

This Fern could handle. 'I think she's very beautiful, also she's lonely and looking for someone to lean on. I'm sure she would make you an excellent wife.'

'Don't I have any say in the matter?' Brett spoke in a quiet voice. 'Lisa is a sweet girl, but I might not like to choose her for my wife. I might prefer an ill-tempered shrew like yourself.'

'That would be your hard cheese.'

'Okay. We'll leave it for now. I'm glad Lisa didn't upset you, and I'm glad to have your full approval to fire ahead with her. Most other girls wouldn't be so generous as to keep wearing my ring while I was taking another girl out and enjoying her kisses. I thought we might have had something

138

going for us, but I must have been mistaken. I mean, if there was I wouldn't want to kiss Lisa, and if you cared for me, you wouldn't be encouraging me to marry Lisa.'

Fern smiled at him; the only sign she gave that his remarks hurt her was that her brown eyes darkened, but then the smile did not reach her eyes. 'You're so right. I'm pleased you're being so sensible. Now having settled everything I wish you'd take yourself off and let me have my lunch.'

'Right, I'll do that. We're still friends, I hope, and you won't hesitate to ask me for anything you need?'

Fern was about to say that there was nothing she wanted, when she remembered the vindictive look in Lisa's eyes as she spoke to Robbie this morning. 'Yes, there is something. Lisa said something about using her influence with you to get Robbie fired. I hope you wouldn't give him his marching orders just on her say-so? Robbie was rude, but there were extenuating circumstances.'

'I give you my word that Lisa will have nothing to do with Robbie staying or leaving. If I sack Robbie it will be because he can't do his work efficiently, and you have to admit that gives me plenty of leeway.'

'Thanks.' Fern sat down and opened her lunch box.

'Robbie seems to have gained our friendship and your loyalty. So if you want his stay to be prolonged, and not abruptly terminated, you can give him a message from me.'

Fern paused in the act of choosing a sandwich, and looked up at Brett apprehensively.

'Just warn him that if I ever hear him referring to me as Brett baby just once, they'll carry him off the farm on a stretcher.'

Fern could have sworn he was laughing as he went up the track. He reached the top and turned to give her a cheerful wave, then disappeared from view.

He didn't like being called 'Brett baby'. It seemed to Fern that she had made a startling discovery. It was so funny, so hilariously funny that she started to laugh and couldn't stop. If there was a touch of hysteria in her laughter it did not worry her, it was much better to laugh than to cry.

The week between Christmas and New Year was not easy for Fern. She avoided meeting Brett and Lisa most of the time. But, of course, Brett came in for meals. In a way Mr. Alexander's health helped her, because he appeared to have shaken off the weakness that had been plaguing him over the past month, and with his new energy wanted Fern to take him driving each afternoon. Kirsty and Brett were overjoyed with his sudden improvement, but Fern kept her own thoughts to herself; she had seen this stage all too often during her years of nursing.

One day when Fern and Mr. Alexander returned from visiting an old friend up the Valley, they entered the lounge to find Brett and Lisa and the children having afternoon tea with Kirsty.

Fern greeted them smiling as if it were an everyday occurrence, but in her heart she felt as if the enemy had invaded her sanctuary. It was fortunate that the children were present, because they were a safe topic of conversation. Sally and Simon had treated the place as Liberty Hall from the day they arrived, so were quite sure of their welcome. It had amused Fern from the first day when 'Me Jack' had presented himself at the door, a reluctant, terrified Sally trailing him, the way they had walked into Kirsty's heart. Even when she spoke to them sharply, they would stand watching her, showing no fear, somehow knowing that under that severe exterior she was as soft as butter towards children. 'Me Jack' was sprawled on Kirsty's knee half asleep, but Sally quickly crossed the room to take Mr. Alexander's hand and lead him to his special chair, and after a struggle removed his shoes and replaced them with slippers.

Lisa was all smiles. 'Mr. Alexander, you've quite stolen my daughter's heart, your name is never off her lips. I'd like to thank you and Kirsty for being so kind to them, but if they're a nuisance to you please let me know.'

Mr. Alexander accepted his cup of tea from Fern. 'Don't worry about them being a trouble to us, Mrs. Tremaine, Fern usually takes care of them when they're here.'

Fern sat down and drank her tea as quickly as politeness would allow. When she stood up Kirsty said, 'Oh, Fern, would you see if Mrs. Tremaine would like a second cup?'

Lisa refused, but Fern saw that Brett was annoyed about something and guessed it was because his uncle and Kirsty insisted on calling Lisa Mrs. Tremaine.

Brett said flatly, 'I've invited Lisa and the children over to dinner tomorrow night.'

'That will be very nice,' Kirsty said courteously but with no warmth in her voice. 'Tomorrow night is New Year's Eve. I thought you and Fern would be going into Hokitika to the fireworks display and see the New Year in at the clock tower.'

Brett frowned. 'I'd forgotten the date, but Fern isn't very keen on local events, so it doesn't matter. She wouldn't come to the Boxing Day sports.'

Fern broke in, 'If you'll excuse me, please, I'll go and change. I promised Robbie I'd help Ross with the cows to-night.'

Brett looked at her sharply, then in a sarcastic voice, 'I'm lucky that you and Robbie are running the farm for me. There's no need for me to run out a work schedule, but it would have been quite in order for one of you to have let me know your arrangements. I'll have a few words to say to Robbie tomorrow.'

Fern was completely taken aback, and her face flushed, 'You'd better have your *few words* with me, because Robbie didn't ask me, I offered. We did ask Ross, and he said it would be quite all right. We couldn't ask you for the simple reason that you were away riding with Lisa, and by the time you returned late for lunch, Robbie had left, and I was out driving with Uncle Hamish. Now, if you'll excuse me?'

Fern left the room with her head high. How dared he

bawl her out in front of Lisa? She changed quickly and went over to join Ross.

When the milking was nearly finished, Ross pointed up at the gate. 'There's the boss. I'd better go and see what he wants.'

Fern never looked up, but carried on working.

Ross came back. 'He wants a word with you, Fern.'

'You can tell him from me that he can drop dead. And tell him he's not my boss.'

Ross grinned, 'How about that? You're a proper little fire-eater. But you can deliver your own messages. Did you two have a bust-up?'

'You might call it that.'

'Hey! You didn't fall out because of Lisa? The wife was saying that she was sure Lisa would split you two, but I said you wouldn't be that silly.'

'I'm not that silly,' Fern replied furiously. 'And as for Alexander the Great, he can wait up there till I'm finished.'

Brett had disappeared by the time Fern finished, which did not improve her temper. She went home and rang Jane Hamilton.

'Hi, Jane. Fern here. Could I by any chance invite myself to dinner at your place tomorrow night?'

'You're welcome any time. They tell me via the grapevine that you've got a cuckoo in the nest. True or false?'

'A bit of each. Actually I don't think you would call her a cuckoo, I think she has probably more right to be here than I do. Still, she doesn't grab me, if you get my meaning, and she's dining here tomorrow night, I thought I'd get me a bolthole.'

'Whatever the reason, you're invited. Say, if you and Brett aren't going out how about joining up with our gang for a night on the town, unless Brett would be mad, that is? Darcy's girl friend is in hospital, and he needs cheering up.'

'Sounds wild. Count me in. See you about six then. 'Bye.'

Fern hung the phone on the hook with a satisfied grin.

After a shower she dressed for dinner, and joined Kirsty in the kitchen. 'Kirsty, you don't mind if I'm not here for dinner on New Year's Eve? I've been invited over to the Hamiltons', and will be going to town with Jane and her cousins.'

'I'm not the one who should be objecting, Fern.'

'Oh, you mean Brett? He's hardly in a position to criticize what I do. If you want me to stay and help at dinner just say so. I'll set the table now.'

Kirsty looked up from carving the meat. 'I'm thinking that's a strange suggestion. You'll stay if I ask you, but not if Brett asked you.'

Fern, busy getting the silver out to set the table, did not answer.

On her next trip back to the cupboard Kirsty spoke again. 'I can manage quite well without you, so away you go and enjoy yourself . . .'

'Enjoy yourself where?' Brett asked as he came in.

Fern did not speak, so Kirsty explained, 'Fern is having dinner with the Hamiltons, and then going to town with them on New Year's Eve.'

'Is she now? Tell me, Kirsty, if I have five minutes with Fern alone, now, would it ruin the dinner?'

Kirsty replied with a smile, 'You can have a quarter of an hour if you like. If you're longer than that Hamish and I will start without you.'

'Right. Fern, put those things down and come outside with me. I want to talk to you, and I don't want to be interrupted.'

Fern's eyes flashed fire. 'That's what I like about you – no invitation, just an order. Well, you may not be hungry, but I am. So go outside and talk to yourself.'

'Please, will you come, Fern? I don't seem to have seen you at all this past few days.'

'And whose fault is that? No, I'm not coming.'

Brett moved towards her. 'I've said please and you still refuse. I'll give you two seconds, and then I'm going to pick you up and carry you. Make your choice.'

'You wouldn't *dare*!' But she knew he would, so she placed the tray down on the table and stalked ahead of him out the front door. She stopped on the steps. 'Is this a stand-up or a sit-down fight?'

'We'll go and sit on the bench in front of the garage,' Brett answered, completely unruffled, and he led the way there. He sat down. 'Have a seat, Fern.'

Fern moved to the opposite end of the bench, and sat down in angry silence.

Brett mocked her gently, 'Something has come between us, Fern . . . say six feet of wooden bench.'

Fern sat woodenly staring straight ahead.

'Listen, Fern. I want to apologize for speaking to you as I did in the lounge today. I went over to the shed to do so, but you wouldn't speak to me. Will you accept my sincere apologies?'

Fern turned to face him, 'No, I will not. That's the third time you've spoken first and regretted afterwards. Twice I've said forget it, but this time I will neither forget nor forgive. You think I'm such a softie that you can say what you like, when you like, and then say "I'm sorry". What you did today was unforgivable – in front of Kirsty and Mr. Alexander too. Before, you saved your most unpleasant remarks for my ears alone.'

'Not to mention in front of Lisa?' Brett remarked.

'Humph! Who cares what you say in front of her? I'm completely indifferent to her opinion of me. But I do not like to be put down in front of Kirsty and your uncle. I care very much what they think of me.'

Brett sighed. 'Their good opinion of you hasn't been tarnished, believe me. I know what I'm talking about. They let me know exactly what they thought of my rudeness to a guest of the house, not to mention my fiancée. As Lisa was there I could hardly point out that their "Frosty Friday" treatment of an old friend was also bad manners, but I was annoyed.'

'That's the understatement of the year,' Fern retorted angrily. 'I wasn't in that room long before I saw you were seething because they called her Mrs. Tremaine. And that is her name, so I don't know why you got so uptight about it. The only reason you bawled me out was that you were fuming because they didn't roll out the red carpet for your Lisa. In my opinion they were courteous and polite, and I'm damned if you could have expected more in the circumstances. You were more clumsy than I could have believed possible . . . ramming her down their throats like that, even allowing for the fact that you're infatuated by her.'

'What do you mean "under the circumstances"? Lisa was almost part of the family when she lived here years ago, so I naturally thought they'd be as pleased to see her as I was.' He glared at Fern.

Fern laughed, 'You're out of sight, really how could you be so *dumb*? I'll give you an example . . . I've been here a couple of months and they've treated me as if I belonged here. Say I left suddenly taking something they value very much with me? Knowing them I doubt if they would set the police on me, but I wouldn't expect to walk back in here a couple of years later and expect to be treated to a warm, friendly welcome.'

'Lisa never took anything that they valued,' Brett protested.

'You've got to be joking! It must have escaped your notice that they love you very dearly, and if someone hurts you, it hurts them too. They blame Lisa for all the years of happiness you could have had, that's what she stole from them. If you'd married Lisa when you came home they would have had the pleasure of seeing you happily married, and more than likely enjoyed watching your family grow up. There's nothing of value in the house that I could take to equal that loss.'

There was a long silence then Brett spoke again. 'I didn't think of it from that angle. I thought because I could forget the past and treat her as a friend that they could naturally do

145

the same. What's that jab about me being infatuated with her?'

'Sorry, that was a bit nasty. You're in love with her, I guess. If you were any sort of a man, you'd tell them and I'm sure they would be quite happy about it. It's just because they think we're serious that they think Lisa is going to mess up your life again. If you told them the truth, that Lisa is the only girl you want, and I gave you back your ring, I'm sure they'd understand. Why, you're half there. They love those kids already.'

'What about you? Wouldn't it upset you if we broke our engagement? I mean, you'd want to leave, and Uncle Hamish wouldn't like that.'

'Why should I be upset?' Fern stared ahead at Kirsty's rose garden, not daring to face Brett. 'I wouldn't have any right to be upset. I've known all along that our engagement is just a game. As for leaving, once you'd explained to Uncle Hamish that I couldn't care less who you married, I think I'd like to stay on, if he wanted that.'

Brett was silent for so long that Fern looked at him. Then he said, 'If you don't object I'll leave things as they are in the meantime. You could be right, but from what Uncle Hamish has said to me, I doubt that he'd be any too pleased if we told him we'd been fooling him all along. I think you'll have to leave it to my judgement.'

Fern felt like a man reprieved from the noose. Even though it hurt to carry on this fake engagement, it would have hurt her a lot more if he had agreed to dropping her for Lisa. But in all honesty she had had to make the offer.

'Right. Whatever you say.' She stood up.

'We haven't finished yet. Why are you going out tomorrow night? Is it because I invited Lisa over? Why wouldn't you go to the sports with me, and yet you'll go with that Hamilton mob tomorrow night?'

Fern, who had been feeling sympathetic towards him, immediately changed back to being furious. 'One, you didn't ask me to go to the sports with you, you announced in front of Lisa that you were taking me. When she wanted to go, I naturally stayed home. Two, I'm not in love with Lisa, and I doubt that she would even miss me tomorrow night. Three, I'm going out on the town with Jane because, Brett baby, I want to live it up on New Year's Eve. If you think entertaining Lisa is all you want, well, go to it, but don't expect me to think it's the social event of the year!'

Brett stood up and looked down at her. 'So I made a blue, but I *would* like you to accompany me to the New Year's dance at Kokatahi the night after that. Everyone goes, and I think you'd enjoy it.'

'Thank you, I'd love to go.' Then a thought struck her. 'I mean, I'd love to go if it's just us two, but if it's a threesome count me out. Is it?'

'Certainly not. Just the two of us. What do you think I am?'

Fern grinned wickedly, 'Don't tempt me!'

The thought that she was going to have Brett to herself tomorrow night for a whole evening added an extra fillip to Fern's enjoyment of New Year's Eve. They were a happy, noisy group, all intent on having a good time, and as Fern reported to Kirsty next morning, 'It was a real gas.'

'And that is good?' Kirsty inquired, noticing how pretty Fern looked.

'Just the best ever,' Fern told her gaily as Brett walked in.

Brett put the milk on the bench. 'And I suppose you're referring to last night. I surmise a dozen chaps kissed you at midnight.'

Fern fluttered her eyelashes coquettishly. 'Not dozens, but hundreds, if not thousands – I didn't count.'

'So one more wouldn't matter?'

'I'd hardly notice it.' Fern's eyes sparkled with fun.

'Good. Happy New Year, Fern darling.' He caught her in his arms and kissed her.

Then he let her go, and said, 'What big eyes you've got, Grandma! Are you surprised that it happens even when there's no moon to magic us? Let me show you again.'

147

Fern ducked away from him. 'You're embarrassing Kirsty.'

Brett followed Fern, teasing her, 'You're not embarrassed, are you, Kirsty?'

As Fern took shelter behind Kirsty, who was smiling broadly, Kirsty put her hand up. 'Now, now, Brett! If Fern says I'm embarrassed, then I must be.'

Brett grumbled, 'You women, sticking together against one poor man! Well, if Fern thinks you're embarrassed then I'll see you are.' He put his arms around Kirsty and kissed her cheek. 'And a Happy New Year to you too, Kirsty darling.'

As he went to the bathroom to wash, Fern asked, 'Can I wish you a Happy New Year too, Kirsty?' And without waiting for permission she kissed Kirsty also. It was then she noticed a tear moving slowly down Kirsty's wrinkled cheek.

'I'll make the tea now, Kirsty,' she said, to give Kirsty time to compose herself. It made her wonder how long it was since Brett had shown his real affection for the old lady, maybe years . . . then she remembered Doctor Walters mentioning that they loved Brett, but were not a demonstrative family.

Fern prepared Mr. Alexander's tray, and carried it down the wide passage. Brett met her half-way. 'Ha! At last I have you alone!'

'You have not, too! I've got Uncle's tray.' She warded him off.

'I'll go along with you and wish him the compliments of the season too.'

'Didn't you do that last night?'

'For your information, I didn't wish anyone anything last night. Lisa went home with the children about eight, and Kirsty and Uncle took themselves off to bed about nine, and I sat and watched TV. until it shut down.'

As Fern greeted the old man and placed his tray in front of him, she kept feeling Brett was trying to tell her something, but it was so tremendous she dared not even guess at it . . . if she was wrong . . . no, of course, she was wrong. He loved Lisa, he had not denied it last night . . . he was just in a crazy mood.

Uncle Hamish had his bright eyes on her. 'You look very chipper this morning, Fern. Like someone who's lost a penny and found a shilling. Did you have a good time last night?'

'Fantastic,' and catching Brett's gaze across the bed she blushed. 'I'll be back for your tray.'

But Brett caught her at the door, and picked her up in his arms. Turning to his uncle, he said, 'If you want to know what gave her such a glorious colour, watch.'

Just before he kissed her, he queried, 'Are you sure you can't tell one man's kiss from another's? I'll guarantee you'll notice the difference this time.'

And she did.

At breakfast he asked, 'What would you like to do today, Fern?'

Fern looked at Kirsty. 'If you've made any plans, I'll fit in with them. But if everyone's doing their own thing I'd like to make myself a dress for tonight.'

Kirsty asked, 'What about your long green frock?'

'Oh, it's a bit formal. Jane and her friends are all wearing the new country-style gear, and if you'll give me the gingham you bought for the new curtains, I could run one up in a matter of hours. I'd replace the curtain stuff next week, if you'd let me?'

'I'm damned if I'll take you to a ball wearing curtains . . .'

'Be quiet, Brett,' Kirsty said firmly. 'Show me a sketch. Get that pencil and paper.'

Quickly Fern drew the simple pattern she intended to use. 'The other girls have lace here at the bodice and at the sleeve here, and I think Jane has a width round about four inches from the hem, like this, but it doesn't have to be too elaborate.'

149

'Now that's a womanly style. Certainly you can have the gingham, and I've got quite a lot of lace, you can sort through it and take what you need.'

'Very rustic,' commented Brett. 'I suppose you won't need any flash jewellery, just stick a straw in your mouth and you'll all look like scarecrows.'

'If you don't want to go with me, I'll get someone else,' Fern threatened.

'Who said I don't want to go with you? I only made a fair comment. I'll wear my very best rustic gear to match. If you ladies are going to be busy all day making dresses, I'm off down to the Kokatahi Gun Club. I'll be back for lunch. Good-bye.'

Fern and Kirsty were so engrossed in conversation they hardly heard him.

'I think I'll shoot myself,' Brett stated.

'That's a good idea, Brett,' Kirsty answered. 'Don't be late for lunch.'

Brett roared laughing and went out, shutting the door behind him. Kirsty and Fern looked at each other, mystified. Fern said, 'Men!' and Kirsty nodded, 'They can be trying.'

As soon as the table was cleared, Fern brought out the gingham and Kirsty put a heap of lace on the end of the table. After a while Mr. Alexander wandered through and sat down on the Colonial couch, content to watch the women working.

By lunch time it was finished, and Fern went to try it on for the last time. This time she made up her face, put sandals on and brushed her long hair smooth and shining, then caught it below each ear with a wide green satin bow. Then fearing that she'd cut the neck too low, she added the Celtic cross. It was perfect.

She went out to the kitchen to show the others. Standing with her hands carefully clasped in front of her, she asked demurely, 'You like?'

Kirsty and Uncle Hamish were full of praise, Uncle about

her appearance, and Kirsty because she had been so quick to sew up the dress. Satisfied, Fern hurried back to her room as she saw Brett coming round the path. He could wait till this evening. She changed into her shorts and top and went out to join them at lunch.

'Don't I get to view the masterpiece?' Brett questioned.

But Fern was adamant. 'No.'

Brett went back to the Gun Club and Fern drove Kirsty and Uncle Hamish up to the Gorge to have a picnic afternoon tea. She had to fight down the rising excitement which came over her each time she thought of the Ball. She was *dumb*. Knowing what she did, and still hoping was stupid. But she couldn't help speculating.

After dinner she changed into her gingham dress, and put on a little more make-up than she had used in the afternoon. She went into the lounge to wait for Brett.

He had changed all right. He was wearing a pair of work shorts that were threadbare and torn, a handkerchief around his neck and heavy hobnailed boots. 'Do I look a proper partner for a scarecrow?'

Kirsty told him just what he looked like in no uncertain terms.

Brett grinned, 'I'm sure Fern wouldn't agree with you. She says it's not the clothes that count, but the person inside them. Isn't that true, Fern?'

Fern giggled, 'I'm ready when you are.'

'You mean it? You'd go with me dressed like this?'

'It'd be a real gas. But you've got to promise not to walk on me with those boots when we're dancing.'

'You know, I think you really would.'

Mr. Alexander spoke in a tone that brooked no contradiction. 'Young man, Fern has spent some time prettying herself up for you, and if she's prepared for you to escort her in those clothes, I am not.'

Brett chuckled, 'But I wasn't thinking of asking you to be my partner.' But he left the room hurriedly.

When he came back he took Fern's hand. 'Let's get out of

here before Uncle sends me back to polish my shoes, and Kirsty scrutinizes my neck to see if I've washed properly. Goodnight, all.'

Brett helped her into the car, and made sure her long skirt wasn't caught in the door. 'You look very sweet tonight, Fern.'

'Thank you kindly, sir. Actually, you don't look too bad yourself.'

'That's praise indeed.'

After that they were silent, but it was a friendly silence.

Inside the hall, Fern waved across the room to Jane. Brett pointed to some empty seats at the far end of the Hall. 'We can go and join Jane and her friends, or we can sit down there by ourselves – say the word.'

'We'll sit by ourselves now, and maybe join the gang later. Okay with you?'

'Very okay.'

The first dance was the Twist, so Fern had no breath to talk. The next was a gorgeous dreamy waltz. 'They cater for all tastes here tonight,' Brett remarked as he drew her into his arms. Fern felt so close to him, not only physically, but mentally, that she didn't dare speak and risk spoiling this precious moment. It was as if this week had never happened, as if this night followed Christmas night.

When they were seated once more, Fern felt brave enough to ask, 'Why are you being so nice to me today?'

'Haven't I been nice to you all the time?'

'Of course you haven't, Brett. So don't dodge the question.' Fern felt she had to know.

'Well, I did a lot of thinking last night. I even tried your suggestion on Uncle, and he threw a pink fit, even though I had made a joke about it to test the ground. So it looks like we'll have to stay together a bit longer. I thought we might as well enjoy it.'

As Fern looked bleakly down the dance floor, she shivered as if ice cold. What a damned fool she'd been! The way she'd jumped at the chance to be friends with him again.

She was pathetic, that was the only word that fitted her behaviour – pathetic.

'Hi, I was looking all over for you, Brett.'

Fern lifted her gaze and saw it was Lisa wearing a slinky black gown that fitted her as if she had been sewn into it. Fern wasn't even surprised to see her. It all went together like a jig-saw puzzle. A kiss in front of Kirsty, to set her mind at rest, a kiss in front of Mr. Alexander to show him everything in the garden was lovely, and she had thought his affection was genuine. How could she have been so crazy, so – so – easy! She writhed inwardly at the thought.

She stood up. 'Have my seat, Lisa. I'm just going over to talk to Jane.'

She never gave Brett one glance. Not that it had been his fault . . . it was all her own wishful thinking. But never again. She avoided Jane and went through to the ladies' powder room. She had to have a few minutes to pull herself together again. She knew she had to go back there, laughing and gay, and pretending she was having a wonderful time. When she heard the music start again she returned to the hall, and joined Jane. 'Hi, everybody. Mind if I join you?'

Darcy, with whom she'd been last night, put his arm around her, and whooped, 'Fern, just the girl I've been waiting for! May I have this dance with you, and book another for later? Once this mob sees you're on the loose I won't get a look in.'

'You can have as many as you want, Darcy.'

'Well, what are we waiting for?'

Jane whispered quietly, 'Is that the opposition?'

Fern nodded.

'Gee, I'm sorry, Fern. I hope she sneezes and then her plunging neckline will become topless, as if it isn't nearly that already. You come back here with Darcy after this dance. You won't have to worry about partners, the boys thought you were great last night.'

Darcy, who had been waiting impatiently just out of ear-shot, said, 'Come on, Fern, you two can yak in between dances.'

Fern followed him on to the floor, smiling. Yes, she would have a good time with Darcy tonight. No chance of getting involved there, he was very much in love with his girl, and most of his conversation consisted of singing her praises. And he was a superb dancer, good-looking, too . . . what more could a girl ask for in a partner?

During the next interval Brett came across the room.

'Fern, I'd like to speak to you, in private, if you'll excuse us.'

Fern moved a small distance away from the group, and stopped. 'Fire away.'

'First, I didn't invite Lisa to the ball, and I didn't know she was coming . . .'

Fern's laughter was a shade brittle. 'You know, that's a good story. I'd stick to it if I were you. I don't know why you feel you should explain yourself to me. It's your uncle and Kirsty you're out to *impress*, and I have to admit that you really were outstanding today – you nearly had me fooled, but not quite.'

'Would you please come back and sit with us? I'll get someone to take her off my hands. I can't walk off and leave her. If you don't it will give cause for comment.'

Fern flared, 'Do me a favour, please . . . Get lost! As for comment, you're a bit late to start worrying, everyone is gossiping already. As for sitting with you and Lisa, you're out of sight, you really are. What are your plans? – one dance with me, and then it's her turn? Grow up, Brett baby, I would share a lot of things with a lot of people, money, clothes, bed and board, even my last crust I'd be willing to share, but one thing I won't share is a man. You'd better believe it.'

She turned away and walked back to Jane. As she moved she thought the bit about the stiff upper lip would be a lot easier to manage than a perpetual grin.

The evening went on and on and on. Fern knew that it was her own fault that the evening was turning into an endurance test. The band was really swinging, the floor glass-smooth, and everyone else was on cloud nine as far as she could guess.

Darcy had been happy to see her back. 'Must be my New Year luck. I thought Brett was going to hijack you.'

'He tried.'

As they were performing a very spirited version of the Canadian Three-Step it wasn't a good time for conversation, which pleased Fern.

Later on, after she had listened to all Anne's perfection, from a delightfully biased Darcy, he hesitated. 'I must be the most boring partner you've ever been forced to spend an evening with?'

Fern laughed with genuine amusement. 'You have a poor opinion of yourself. It's somewhat rare to find anyone so unashamedly in love with a girl. I think it's beautiful. If I had the pick of the hall I'd have chosen you ... I don't feel much like talking, and you're interesting and easy to listen to, I love dancing and you're a super partner. Feeling better?'

'Much. About dancing – that's the only thing we haven't got in common – Anne, I mean.'

'I'd never have guessed,' Fern teased. 'Doesn't she like dancing?'

'Worse, she can't dance, and she refuses to let me teach her.'

Fern replied, 'If I couldn't dance I'd be darned if I'd let my boy-friend teach me. What, and let him know how clumsy I was? However, if I loved him very much and knew he wanted to dance with me I'd be inclined to go to a school of dancing and have a few lessons.'

'Do you think she would? I could pay for the lessons, sort of give it to her for a birthday present. Do you think she'd be upset?'

'She's your girl-friend, work it out for yourself. If you maybe dropped a hint about some mutual acquaintance who has become a wonderful dancer through having a few lessons, she may grab at the chance. It would be better if she believed that she'd thought it up herself. Then she would try all the harder to give you a pleasant surprise.'

'You know, you're not only a pretty face, you've got brains. And you don't look clever, either,' Darcy said with a smile.

'Flatterer!'

'You know, I was only kidding. You've helped me with something that was a worry, how about letting me return the favour? You're still wearing Brett's ring, so you must be still engaged to him, but here you are spending the evening with me. Not that I'm complaining, mind, but Brett's a great chap, and if it's just a silly tiff, maybe I could act as go-between and fix it up. If I'm talking out of turn, just slap me down.'

'You're right on all counts, he's a great guy, I'm wearing his ring, and we're still engaged, and we've had not a tiff but a flaming great row, and I appreciate your offer of peace-maker but I would rather fight my own battles. Now we'll forget all about it and talk about your Anne.'

'If that's the way you want it, okay. I'm booking you up for every dance except the last one.'

Fern pretended to be hurt. 'Don't you think you will last the course?'

Darcy explained hurriedly, 'The last dance here is special as far as the locals are concerned. You only dance the last dance with someone you care for, like a husband and wife, or engaged couples, or if you're going steady. Even perhaps if you've only met a girl here tonight, and you've sort of clicked, you often see the start of a new romance during the last waltz of the New Year's Ball. It doesn't count if you come from town, only if you live in the district. You'll see all those older couples up on the floor, and believe me, they could dance most of us young ones off the floor.'

'I think it's a lovely custom. If you're not dancing the last waltz, I'll go out to the car as well.'

The next dance was a Veleta, and everyone kept changing

156

partners. Inevitably she met Brett and he stated, 'You'll save the last dance for me.'

'I've heard about the tradition of the last waltz, and I think you should dance it with Lisa; it would bring back many happy memories. I'll be out in the car waiting for you.'

As she changed partners again she was angry to find her hands were shaking. He had no right to order her around. He never asked, not Alexander the Great, he just expected everyone to fall in with his wishes.

When the M.C. called, 'Ladies and gentlemen, take your par ... s for the last dance, if you please,' Fern and Darcy started towards the door, after saying goodnight to the others in the party, as they swung two by two on to the floor.

'I'll drive you home if you like, Fern. I've got to go past your place anyway,' Darcy offered.

Fern looked and said gratefully, 'Thanks. That will be marvellous.' Anything to get out of this hall and not witness Brett and Lisa having their special dance.

A crowd blocking the door halted their progress, and Fern felt despair as Brett put his hand on Darcy's shoulder. 'Thanks for minding my girl for the night, but it's the last dance, and we're having it together.'

Fern said stubbornly, 'I'm not dancing with you, and I'm going home with Darcy.'

Brett stood there smiling down at her. 'I'm sure Darcy isn't looking for any trouble. You're not disputing my right to have the last dance with Fern?'

Darcy shrugged his shoulders. 'It's between you and him, Fern. See you.'

Fern went to follow him, but Brett took her arm in a vice-like grip. 'If you're begging for a fight you are going to get it, Fern. Either you come with me willingly on to the dance floor, or I'll pick you up in my arms and waltz round the floor with you ... that will give them something to talk about for years!'

'What are you hoping to prove, Muscle Man?' She was so mad she could have screamed, but rather than make a scene she went with him on to the dance floor.

Not a word was spoken as they circled the room. Fern tried to hold him at arm's length, but he pulled her close and held her. 'Watch it, Fern baby. You don't know how close you've been to getting a thoroughly deserved spanking this evening, but if you try me any more you're going to get it.'

Fern could not speak, she was so seething. She needed a spanking? She did? Oh, he really was something else!

On the trip home she sat as far away from him as she could. When he stopped the car in front of the house, she was out in a flash and running up the steps. He did not try to follow her, but drove on into the garage.

She was trembling as she removed her make-up. How dared he humiliate her like that ... oh, she could kill him! He was trying to put her in the wrong. How like a man!

One day he was going to get his, he had it coming. And Fern only hoped she was there to see it.

CHAPTER NINE

On the Sunday following New Year's Day Brett was called to the phone about mid-morning. Fern ignored him as he went through to his office; she had been ignoring him ever since the ball. What annoyed her most of all was the fact that he didn't seem to be aware that he *was* being ignored, or if he did know, he didn't let it bother him. As for keeping up a face in front of Kirsty and Mr. Alexander, Fern thought that they had been given enough reassurance to last them to the end of the month.

Kirsty made a cup of tea. When Brett came in they were all seated round the table. He was obviously pleased with himself.

'What do you know?' he announced. 'My jet boat is ready. Jim's just finished tuning her up and is bringing her out here this afternoon. Fern, would you like to be my first passenger? I'll try her out after lunch. You'll come?'

'No, thanks.'

'Why not?' Brett's blue eyes were full of mischief. 'Uncle, do you think Fern needs an afternoon off? She works far too hard. Kirsty, I'll leave you to persuade her, but I do think it's important that she comes with me. Don't you?'

He swallowed his tea hastily, and went out.

'It will do you the world of good, Fern,' Kirsty stated firmly. 'You'll enjoy it. Brett has had a boat for several years, but it wasn't until last year that I gained the courage to go with him on the river. I was a small bit nervous, but Brett is a good driver, and handles his boat skilfully. It gives you a completely new picture of the countryside. Now, I won't hear any more argument! You agree, Mr. Hamish?'

'What are you scared of, Fern? The worst that can happen is you might have to swim for it, but it's a nice day.' Mr. Alexander continued, 'I think it's quite an honour to be chosen for the maiden voyage. Brett has been waiting for the boat to arrive, and it's natural that he wants to show it off to you. He lent his other jet to some friends making a trip up the Bullet Gorge last year, and it was swamped and sank without a trace. Well, that's settled, you'll go.'

'Yes, I'll go,' Fern said, but her voice lacked enthusiasm. That Brett was downright sneaky ... he knew she would refuse him so he'd set the other two on to her. She'd go all right, but she wouldn't enjoy it ... not even if it meant sitting the whole journey with her eyes shut.

While she was putting the lunch dishes away she saw in the drive the Landrover towing a trailer on which rode a jet boat. She couldn't help feeling a little thrilled at the thought of the trip. The boat was spanking new, gleaming paint, and every curve and line of it fairly shouted speed.

When Brett called, she went out thinking she must might enjoy the new experience. After all, there was no use in cutting off her nose to spite her face. She arrived by the boat at the same time as Lisa. She listened to Lisa's praise of the smooth sleek lines, and knowledgeable talk about the engine, showing that what she didn't know about jets wasn't worth mentioning.

Fern did a slow burn, as she waited for the spiel to finish. How come Lisa always knew the right thing to say – mention a boat and she rattled off non-stop about engines, mention a horse and away she went about sires, lines and studs, mention a dog and she was off about eye dogs, huntaways, blue heelers and Kelpies. And Smithy thought she was a *dumb* blonde!

Lisa was flushed with excitement and Fern had to admit she was devastating, sparkling, vivacious, and saying exactly the right things to please Brett. No wonder he couldn't resist her.

'Are you going for a run now? Please, pretty please, can little Lisa go with you?'

'Sorry, the first trip is reserved for Fern,' Brett turned her down with a smile.

Jim reversed the Landrover and trailer out of the drive, and headed towards the bridge.

'Please, Fern, can I go in your place? It would mean so much to me, and you can go another time.'

Brett shook his head. 'Cut it out, Lisa. You can go next time.'

Lisa pouted her pretty red lips, and then gave in gracefully. 'Whatever you say, darling. But there's no reason why I can't go down to the river with you, is there?'

'None that I can think of . . . now I'll get the car.'

When he stopped the car beside them, Fern said to Lisa, 'Hop in. I've changed my mind about going. In fact, I wasn't very keen in the first place.'

Lisa needed no second bidding. She got in beside Brett, then wound down the window and called, 'Seeing you're going to be staying at home would you mind giving my car a wash and polish? The roads here are shockingly dusty.'

Brett switched the motor off. 'You leave that car alone! Lisa, you've got one hell of a nerve . . . Fern isn't on the payroll, you know, she's a guest here, like yourself.'

Lisa answered sulkily, 'I didn't say she had to do it, and if you're going to kick up such a commotion, I'll get Robbie to do it when I get back.'

Brett was furious, and Fern laughed. Lisa really was something! The sheer blatant nerve of her taking Fern's place, then ordering her to wash the car, then seeing it annoyed Brett, changing to Robbie. One thing was clear, Lisa had no intention of doing the job herself.

Brett got out of the car, and shouted, 'Fern, you get right back in the car when I tell you, or . . .'

Fern laughed again. '. . . Or you'll what? Dragging me on to the dance floor by force is one thing, but holding me down while you steer the boat is another. Perhaps you'd prefer to tie me up. Cheer up, man. Nobody likes a sore loser.' She sketched a mock salute and took off for Smithy's house.

Smithy shouted for her to come in when she knocked. Smithy was mending men's working trousers. 'If there's one

thing I hate about being a farmer's wife, it's patching ...
Yuk! I reckon I was born out of my time. Now, in the
cavemen days, life must have been much more simple
then ... no trousers, and best of all no barbed wire fences
to rip their little fur skin suits on.'

Fern sat down on the sofa and was immediately mobbed
by Sally and Simon.

Smithy yelled, 'Here, you kids, give Fern a fair go. Hey,
Fern, what *are* you doing here? I thought Brett was taking
you up river in his new boat. Don't tell me you let Lisa con
you out of it?' She pushed the pile of mending aside. 'Out,
out you go, you brats! I'm going to have a heart-to-heart
with Fern here. Time somebody did. You great big softie,
you ... when are you going to stand up and fight ... letting
her walk all over you!' She took some biscuits and two
apples. 'Come on now, kids. Here, take these things and beat
it. Don't leave the garden, now. I'll call you when I've
finished with Fern. Sally, keep an eye on Simon.'

'Me Jack' Simon snuggled closer to Fern. Fern kissed
him. He really was gorgeous. 'Your bribery and corruption
hasn't worked, Smithy. Watch me use a little child psychology on them.'

She walked to the door with 'me Jack' still clinging like a
limpet. 'Now, if you both go outside while I talk to Smithy,
I'll take you for a swim, but not if I hear you fighting. Jack,
will you be a good boy?'

'Me Jack. Me good. Me swim.'

Fern kissed him, then put him down with an affectionate
smack on the bottom.

'You debbil child, and you know it. Now, Sally, have we a
deal?' She picked Sally up and cuddled her. Somehow this
fragile little girl caught painfully at her heart-strings. 'Me
Jack' would never be crushed, but Sally?

'Could you read us some more about Winnie the Pooh,
too?' Sally blushed scarlet at her own temerity.

Fern gave her a quick kiss and a hug. 'My, you are coming
on, child! I'm proud of you. If you didn't ask you don't get

in this funny old world of ours. Right, a swim and then two more chapters of Pooh Bear and Rabbit.'

As they ran off, Fern thought regretfully that even if you asked there were some things you didn't get. Now she had to listen to Smithy have her say. Bless her heart, but to Fern it was like rubbing at a sore spot, it didn't help to have the situation talked over and over.

Always there came to her that picture of Brett and Lisa with the children that first morning. They had been so happy, Brett would make a wonderful father for those kids, and no one could deny they needed one. Another picture that seemed to come again and again was the afternoon she had found Lisa and the children at afternoon tea, with 'Me Jack' asleep on Kirsty's knee. It would mean so much to her to have those children to fill the huge emptiness that would come when Hamish Alexander died. Then this afternoon, Lisa doing everything a wife should do, building Brett's ego up, pretty and charming, and not the least of her charm was the 'whatever you say, darling' touch.

Fern sighed; she had nothing to match what Lisa could offer, so how could she stand up and fight for herself, when she wasn't even sure that for her to stay here would be worse for them all in the long run? Her brothers were right, she was a mouse . . . a right rotten mouse.

Smithy placed a mug of coffee in front of Fern and sat down opposite her. 'I don't care if you've had lunch, you're going to need something strong and sweet after my shock treatment.'

Fern grinned at her.

'Take that cheeky grin off your face. You've got nothing to smile about. Robbie told me you had a plan, and we've sat back waiting to see it work. It's not what I'd call a plan, it's a flaming disaster. Lisa is taking Brett over, and you're getting pushed further and further into the background. Wake up, girl . . . do something!'

Fern shrugged her shoulders, then sipped her coffee, her expressive brown eyes still on Smithy's indignant face.

'Stop that, Fern! The position is what I'd call critical. Some plan . . . you go to the ball with Brett, and she dances with him all night . . .'

Fern defended herself, 'He had the last dance with me, and around here that's regarded as of paramount importance.' She thought it was a bit low to claim that as belonging to her plan because it had all been of Brett's choosing.

'Yes, I'll grant you that,' Smithy nodded her head thoughtfully, 'but I still can't see why you let her get away with it. You made it so easy for her.'

Fern sipped her coffee again while she vainly tried to think of an answer to Smithy. Suddenly a bright idea flashed into her mind. She tried to look very wise and knowing. 'It's not always the easy game that attracts the hunter.'

Fern held her breath while Smithy considered the statement.

'Yes. Y-e-s, you could be right. She's always available whenever he wants her, and sometimes when he doesn't, while you play hard to get. You're a deep one, Fern Fraser.'

Fern let out her breath thankfully. She wished she was a deep one, but she wasn't . . . she loved Brett, and . . .

Smithy broke into her thoughts. 'It could be very dangerous if it didn't work. A little give and take is all right, but you're doing all the giving, and Lisa is doing all the taking. Is that part of your plan too?'

Fern nodded. Having no plan whatsoever, she was happy to have Smithy enlarge on her first bright thought. Happy, but a little ashamed of herself for kidding Smithy who was so concerned.

'You know, Fern, it sounds better and better. It's not the way I'd have chosen to handle Lisa, but you're a lot cleverer than me. Brett was saying you were a nurse, so I suppose you learned a lot of psychology and all that stuff. You know, the more I hear these clever dicks going on about it, the more I'm convinced it's just plain old-fashioned common sense.

Take you with the kids a minute ago, you used bribery just the same as me, but you knew what they wanted most ... I suppose that's all there is to it, knowing what they want.'

'Something like that,' Fern agreed. 'Tell me, how do you know so much about the ball? You and Ross weren't there, and Robbie and Maureen were at a private party.'

'The day I have to go to a dance to find out what happened ... well, that'll be the day! The phone keeps you in touch with what goes on, as well as being up to date with most things on the home front.'

Fern decided it was wiser to keep quiet, than ask a question; after all, Smithy was on a party line.

'You see, I was having a snore off the other day, and Lisa must have thought I was out, the place was so quiet. My door was open – I mean, I wasn't listening in on purpose and she said ...'

'I don't want to hear what she said when she thought she was alone,' Fern protested.

'Well, my lady, you're going to hear it whether you like it or not. If it were just idle gossip I wouldn't bother repeating it, but when it concerns the welfare of those across the road, I think you should know.'

Fern didn't know how to stop her, but stood up, preparing to leave.

'Sit down! Lisa was talking to her friend. She said when she married Brett Kirsty would have to leave the farm. She said she would make that one of the conditions before she'd agree to marry him. She said she didn't mind what he spent on the old girl, just as long as he parked her in a flat a good distance away from here.'

'She couldn't! Oh, Smithy, you must have misunderstood her ...'

'I did not misunderstand that little madam. I've seen you watching Brett and those kids, and I knew what a sentimental little goose you are. In fact, I thought they were the reason why you weren't trying very hard to interest Brett.

Of course, now you've told me about the plan, I can see I was wrong. But you should know this and realize it's not only your happiness that's at stake, but also Kirsty's. Can you imagine her in a flat in Christchurch?'

'Yes, unfortunately I can. It would kill her. Oh, I wish you hadn't told me.'

'I suppose you do. I'm going to tell you one more thing and then I'll let you go. Shut up,' Smithy waved aside Fern's anxious objections. 'I want you to know what you're up against. You think you're playing some sort of game with rules like honesty, etc., but believe you me, when Lisa plays, it's for keeps, and she's not above twisting someone's words or telling a downright lie ... no Queensberry rules for that one. She doesn't even regard you as a danger, you're nothing. She told her friend that you and Brett only got engaged to please the old man, and that when he dies you're leaving. Now I know that's a filthy lie, I was here the day you became engaged, I know Brett loves you. I've never seen him so happy for years. Why, at dinner that night, he positively enjoyed Ross's jokes about another good guy gone west. He was so darned proud ...' Smithy's face crumpled. 'And to think I was the blithering idiot that brought her here! If she breaks you two up I'll never forgive her or myself.'

Fern tried to cheer Smithy up, but she was feeling so sick inside herself that she made very little progress. Brett had told Lisa about the engagement after he'd warned her not to tell anyone, and had given his word on it.

'The kids are waiting for me to take them swimming, Smithy. You hop off to bed, and have a rest while I've got them away from the house. And don't worry yourself or blame yourself. If Lisa can split Brett and me then it wasn't much of an engagement to start with, see.'

The words nearly choked her, but she didn't cry. Her eyes were dry and painful, and her throat had a huge lump in it. Why couldn't she cry? She longed for the earlier days when the tears had poured down her cheeks at the least provocation. Now she wanted the relief of tears there were not any.

'You kids ready? Golly, you've got your togs on already. Sally, run over to the line and get my bikini. If I go Kirsty might call me, and I wouldn't get to take you for a swim.'

Sally ran off importantly while 'Me Jack' made vigorous but ineffectual attempts to catch a butterfly.

Sally came puffing back, waving the bikini. 'I saw Kirsty, but she didn't see me. Come quick, Fern, or she may stop us.'

As they neared the river, Fern heard the full-throated roar of the jet boat going back down river. The children raced down the track, but were disappointed at missing it. Fern was not disappointed. She played and fooled with the children for about an hour, then they went back to Smithy's.

Sally ran ahead. 'I'll get the book, I'll get the book!'

'Don't wake Smithy if she's lying down. Be quiet now, Sally.' But she need not have worried; as she neared the door she heard the angry whirr of the sewing machine. 'Hi! We're back, Smithy. I thought you were going to bed.'

'I've nearly finished these pants. It's amazing what you can accomplish when you're in a temper.

'I see the others have just come back from the boat. Lisa is going inside with Brett,' she reported a few minutes later.

Fern didn't answer; there was nothing to say. She was amazed how steady her voice was as she read to the children. She even got the right tones for the different animals. She had just read the last page when Lisa came in. They were pleading for more.

Fern shut the book. 'I'm off home. You can read some to Jack, Sally.'

Sally said sadly, 'I can't read as good as you. Jack doesn't like it when I read it to him, and I don't like it too.'

Lisa waited till Fern stood up. 'Really, Fern, I thought you'd know better! Fancy inside and reading on such a lovely day. The children should be outside enjoying the sun and fresh air. You should have gone with Brett, we had a super time. Make me a cup of tea, please, Smithy, I'm whacked.'

'Make it yourself, Lisa. I'm busy,' Smithy retorted sharply. 'Going now, Fern love? Thanks for coming over.'

Fern waved and went out the door. She wished she hadn't gone to Smithy's. She didn't want to be the instrument which would send Kirsty away from the farm. It was too big a load to carry. She knew she'd lost. Brett wouldn't have told Lisa the secret unless he intended to marry her. She didn't want to think of Brett. Not now, not ever. She sat on the garden seat, not thinking, just sitting, her elbows on her knees, her face cupped in her hands, staring blankly down the rose garden, not thinking, not seeing, just being.

It was quite a time before the angry raised voices penetrated and even longer to recognize that they were Brett's and Mr. Alexander's. She stood up and hurried towards the front door. What was Brett thinking about, storming at his uncle like that . . . Dear God, stop them before any damage is done. Brett will never forgive himself if his uncle has a heart turn.

Even then she hesitated at the door . . . they mightn't like her butting in . . . It might stop now. She leant her hot cheek against the door jamb. Please let them stop.

Mr. Alexander was shouting, 'I tell you, I saw it myself. Fern didn't tell me. There she was as bold as brass, riding Gypsy. And you, you great buffoon, had given her permission. That's my horse, and while I'm alive no one but Fern will ride her . . .'

'You're not being fair. Lisa is a better rider than Fern.'

'I know it all. I know that you took Fern to the ball, and you danced all night with that woman. You pretended you were taking Fern on the boat, and it was just a rotten cover-up. You intended to take Lisa all the time. Well, what sort of man are you? I thought you were something fine, something special, but you're not. A real man would never humiliate the girl he was going to marry. Not the way you've treated Fern.'

Fern was crying now, quietly and painfully. So this was to be the end of her visit, setting Brett and his uncle against each other.

She wiped her eyes, and marched into the room; this had gone far enough.

Mr. Alexander was clutching his chest, and leaning on a chair for support. 'Get away from me! You ring my solicitor and have him get out here now. I won't die until I've changed my will. Her kids are not going to inherit this place, your children can . . .'

Fern reached him as he fell. Immediately the nurse took over and the forlorn girl was gone. 'Brett, help me lift him on to the settee – gently now. Good, I'll take it from here. Ring Dr. Walters, tell him what happened and listen carefully to his instructions. Go on!'

She found the heart tablets she was searching for in his top pocket. 'Get me a glass of water, Kirsty, please, then pillows and a rug. He mustn't be moved again till the doctor gets here. Thanks.' She took the glass of water. 'Oh, good, you're awake again, Uncle. You had a bit of a turn, so now lie quietly. I want you to try and swallow this pill. That's good, don't be frightened, everything is all right. I'll look after you, and Dr. Walters is on his way. Now lie back, that's good. Just rest.'

Brett came back from the telephone, his face white under his tan. 'How is he?'

'He's fine, just fine. I've given him a pill . . . it's all right, Uncle, it's only Brett. Take his hand, Brett, he's trying to say something, and he won't rest till he's said it.'

Brett took the small withered hand in his. 'It's Brett.'

Mr. Alexander held Brett's hand tightly. 'Sorry, boy, my fault.'

Brett's voice was husky. 'No, I'm sorry, too.' A muscle quivered in his cheek. Fern was watching her patient. 'I think he's asleep now, Brett. Keep a hold of his hand, it will give him confidence if he wakes up.' She glanced again at her watch. 'What did Dr. Walters say ... you did get him?'

'He said one pill immediately, the ones he carries with him, and another in a quarter of an hour. He's on his way.'

'Good. He's had one now. Oh, thanks, Kirsty.' She took the rug from her and the pillows, and placed them as she had been taught in hospital. There was nothing to do but wait.

She saw Kirsty's face, grey and strained.

'Kirsty, please pour two brandies, and bring them to me.' Fern took Mr. Alexander's pulse again. Her face gave nothing away. A nurse must remain calm, serene and confident.

'Thank you, Kirsty. Drink one yourself, and give one to Brett.'

Kirsty hesitated, and Brett shook his head.

'Drink it up, Kirsty. You've had a bad shock, and you may have to help with nursing tonight. That's good. Now could you please make us all a cup of tea?'

Kirsty swallowed her brandy obediently and went out to make a cup of tea that nobody wanted. But Fern knew that Kirsty would feel better if she felt she was doing something to help. With luck Dr. Walters would be here before the kettle boiled.

'Brett, please drink this. It will help you, and it may be a long night tonight.'

He took the glass from her, and swallowed its contents in one gulp. He did not speak. Fern glanced again at her watch. She took one pill from the bottle and then shook Hamish gently. 'Wake up, Mr. Alexander, time for another pill. There now, swallow it down – here's the water. Swallow it. Good, now you can go back to sleep.' She took his pulse again, and thought it had a fairly strong beat, if somewhat erratic. For the first time, she felt that he might make it. It was a slim chance ...

Dr. Walters drove up and seemed to move from his car to the settee in one movement, in spite of his weight and age.

'Brett, I'd like a couple of minutes with your uncle and

the nurse. Please shut the door on your way out. Take Kirsty with you.'

'Right, Fern. Tell me what you know, clearly and concisely.' He listened attentively, then called on her to help him with tests he must do.

As she obeyed him, Fern recognized yet again the relief she felt at the sight of a doctor, coming up the ward in the lonely night duties, when she was nursing.

Mr. Alexander woke again briefly. 'You're not to take me to hospital. I want your word on that. I want to die in my own bed.'

'You're not going to die if I can help it, Hamish. I've a few more fees to collect from you. If you don't want to go to hospital, that's it, you have my word.'

Hamish went back to sleep.

'Bring those two in now, Fern.'

He stood looking down at Mr. Alexander until they came in, and then moved over to the fireplace. He knocked out his pipe, then slowly filled it and lit it with a match. He drew on the pipe twice, and then spoke. 'As far as I can ascertain, Hamish has had a small heart attack. I'd like to get him into hospital to run a few checks on him, but he's set on staying in his own bed. I gave him my word, and I'll keep it. Perhaps in a couple of days he may not be so reluctant, and we'll take him in then. You two both know what's ahead of him, he could go in a few minutes, or tonight, or not for weeks. With Fern here I'm prepared to leave him. Moving him now may upset him, and do more harm than good. What are your feelings, Brett? Would you prefer he stayed or would you rather I sent an ambulance out for him?'

Brett's colour had returned as the doctor spoke. 'I'd want him home if at all possible. Providing Fern is willing to stay?'

'I'll take that as read. And I can assure you she is a very competent and efficient nurse. You were fortunate she was here. You, Kirsty, speak up. Here, or in hospital? There is a risk, you know.'

171

'Whatever Mr. Hamish wants,' Kirsty answered un-hesitatingly.

'Right, everything's settled. Fern, you go ahead and pre-pare the bed. Brett will carry him there as soon as you're ready. Kirsty, will you go and brew up, and when he's in his own bed, I'll give you your instructions, Nurse.'

For a whole week Fern rarely left his room. She had a bed moved in and slept lightly, unless Kirsty or Brett were tak-ing their turn to sit by him. The doctor called every day, the first time to bring all she would need for specialling a heart patient, even a wheelchair to take him through to the toilet and back. His improvement was rapid and he soon became impatient to be up and about. Finally, Doctor Walters per-suaded him to go into hospital for two days for a check-up. Dr. Walters was an old hand at the game. He cunningly exaggerated Fern's exhaustion from nursing Hamish throughout the past week. He wanted him in hospital so that Fern could have a rest and catch up on her sleep.

'I'm not going in the ambulance. If you want me, you can take me in your car now. But I'm only going for Fern's sake, she's been a grand girl to me, and no doubt to the others.'

As Brett took him out to the car he kept growling, 'This old coot just wants me for a guinea-pig, so he can try out all his new gadgets. But I'll be back. You look after Fern, Brett. And get all this damned junk out of my room before I get back, or there'll be trouble.'

Fern sat at the table after Mr. Alexander had left. Her face had a fine-drawn look. 'It's been a long week,' she sighed as if too tired to go on.

Brett answered, 'It has indeed. Drink your tea, and off you go to bed. I promised Uncle I would look after you, and I mean to do just that. You were in charge when he was sick, but now I'm the boss. You'll do as I say.'

Fern gave a wan smile.

Brett continued, 'Kirsty wants me to say how much we

appreciate your presence here, and your kindness to Uncle Hamish. I'll never forget it.'

'Aren't you going to pay me for all that hard work?' Fern managed a proper smile this time.

'I am not.'

'Good, I see you're learning. I will go to bed, if you don't mind, Kirsty. I think I'll sleep the clock round, so don't wake me for meals, please.'

Kirsty agreed reluctantly. 'For today only. You must eat your meals. I don't know what Mr. Hamish will say when he comes home. Your clothes are just hanging on you.'

'I'll eat like a horse, Kirsty, but not today.' Fern walked down to her room thoughtfully. It wasn't the nursing which made her lose weight, but those long nights with too much to think about.

Next morning she was surprised to see the sun when she woke. She showered and dressed, then went out to the kitchen. 'And a fine large morning it is, Kirsty. Have you been through to the hospital yet?'

Kirsty's face was wreathed in smiles. 'Mr. Hamish will be home tomorrow. The tests were ... what did they say ... oh, yes. "Much as they expected". When I think about what would have happened had you not been here when he had the first attack ... Fern, I'm so very, very grateful. I know you don't want thanks, but I had to say it. You took charge so calmly that it helped Brett and me to keep our heads instead of panicking.'

Fern said with a smile, 'Somehow the picture of you and Brett panicking is hard to conjure up. If I hadn't been there you would have rung Dr. Walters and followed his instructions. I'm glad I was there to help, but don't feel under a load of obligation to me. I only did what any nurse would do in similar circumstances.'

Brett came in. 'Hi, Fern. Did Kirsty tell you the good news? Great, isn't it? You look wonderfully refreshed. I'm riding over the Hokitika river, up past your favourite creek,

Harris Creek. I have to ride over the block to assess what improvement it needs, and trim it down to what I can afford. Would you like to ride with me?'

'I'd love to.' Fern looked at him outlined in the doorway, and knew she would carry this moment in her mind for ever. He was tall and rangy, wearing only shorts and sandals, and tanned almost the colour of deep mahogany. The wind gently ruffled his thick black hair, but it was the light in his eyes that Fern knew she would never see again. It was gratitude and respect, and perhaps tenderness. Fern knew it for what it was, she had seen that look in the eyes of a patient's family many times before. She had always taken it as a tribute to the nursing profession, not to herself personally, but just this once she would take it for herself and hold it in her heart.

'I thought you might, so I've saddled Gypsy. We've nearly finished the haymaking while you've been caring for Uncle. Robbie will mow the last paddock today. We've been very lucky with the long spell of dry weather, it will break soon. Tomorrow we'll put the last lot in, and it feels good to have a full barn and then some. We'll have to see Fern has a good breakfast, it'll be a long day.'

Fern made the tea while Kirsty served the breakfast. Fern wanted to say something to Kirsty and this was the best moment, before Brett returned.

'Kirsty, I know you heard most of the quarrel between Brett and Mr. Alexander last Saturday. I hope you'll believe me when I tell you that everything Brett was accused of was my doing. He wanted me to dance with him that night, but I was mad at him, and he didn't ask Lisa to go on the river with him, in fact, he refused to take her, but I was still angry, so I pushed her into the car and ran off. As for Lisa riding Gypsy, Brett was telling the truth, she *is* a much better rider . . .'

Kirsty held up her hand. 'That's enough, Fern. I know you and I know Brett, and whatever you may think I'm neither deaf nor blind. You mustn't blame yourself for what happened, and I won't blame you, nor will I blame Brett. I love and trust you both. Ah, there you are, Brett, breakfast is on the table.'

Fern ate her breakfast with a hearty appetite. That was one thing behind her. Kirsty was a dear to be so understanding. Uncle Hamish had reacted in the same way when she'd told him a few days ago. She had a feeling Brett also would go along with her suggestions. That was why she was so pleased to be having the day with him. She had thought it all out through this last week, and knew exactly what she had to do. Brett was planning to marry Lisa, but after the quarrel last week there could be no question of telling Mr. Alexander. There was no reason on earth why she couldn't be friends with Brett, now. Friendship might be second best, but it was better than nothing.

Brett and Fern rode all morning, checking the boundary fences. Fern listened with interest as he explained what he hoped to accomplish, and how he would set about it.

When the sun was directly above them, Brett suggested they take their lunch up the old mill track. Fern sat relaxed and easy in the saddle while Gypsy picked her way delicately up the old abandoned tram track. When Brett stopped, so did Gypsy. Fern looked around while Gypsy drank thirstily from the little mountain stream which crossed their path, then disappeared over the steep hundred-foot drop in a gleaming, glistening waterfall.

After tying the horses and loosening the girth straps, Brett led the way to the edge of the bluff, and sat down. 'Great view of the farm you get up here. Share this black pine stump with me?'

Fern sat down and opened her lunch packet, while trying to pick out familiar spots on the farm that lay spread out in front of them. The chorus of the native birds, tuis and bellbirds and the whirrr of the pigeon wings made beautiful background music to the babble of the stream and the muted roar of the waterfall.

As Fern finished her lunch she glanced at Brett and his

blue eyes caught and held hers. Fern was again the first to look away. She bent to pick up a twig. 'Brett, you're always wanting to take me off and ear-bash me. Will you listen to me having my say?'

'Shoot.'

'Well, here goes. The day Uncle had his heart turn I found out a few things I would rather not have known.'

'Such as?' Brett didn't sound angry, just encouraging her to speak.

'Brett, what will happen to Kirsty when you marry?'

'Nothing. Why should it?'

'Say your wife didn't like Kirsty, and I suppose it's only fair to think that a new wife would want her house to herself?'

'We're not talking about you, I presume?' Fern shook her head, and he continued, 'Kirsty will more than likely stay with us, but if she couldn't get along with my wife, then I'd have to make some other arrangements. One thing I could do would be to build a small cottage near the pines. She'd be close enough for me to keep an eye on, and yet independent. However, it's a hypothetical question, and I somehow feel the girl I marry will get along fine with Kirsty.'

A fat lot he knew! 'You'd never let her be sent to town to those pensioners' flats? I know they're quite nice, but Kirsty is too old to take to town life.'

'You're a funny little thing. All this concern for Kirsty, all of a sudden! You should know me well enough by now to realize she'll be well looked after, always.'

Fern knew Brett was watching her, but she kept her eyes on the river away in the distance. 'Yes, I suppose I do. But it's always nice to be reassured.'

'Yes, it is, isn't it, Fern?'

Fern heard the amusement in his voice, but she was determined not to be sidetracked. She had to get it all out now, while she still had this curious detached feeling, probably the result of a week in almost solitary confinement.

'I've explained to your uncle and to Kirsty that it was my

fault, all those stupid things he was quarrelling about.'

'Were they happy to blame you instead of me?' Brett asked.

'Not exactly. Kirsty said she loved and trusted us both, and she didn't think anyone was to blame, just force of circumstances. Uncle Hamish was just as understanding.'

'That was very thoughtful of you, Fern, to try and clear my name. Thank you.'

Again the merest hint of laughter in his voice.

Fern bent foward, letting her hair fall forward to screen her face. 'I know you're going to marry Lisa, when I leave here. I think it's a bit hard on the two of you to carry on as if there was nothing between you.' Fern cleared her throat, and carried on, 'I'm prepared to help you all I can . . . I mean if you want to use me as a cover, that's okay. I've been a bit stupid, but I know what I'm doing now. If you like, I'd be happy to consider you a good friend, and hope you'll feel the same towards me.

'I know we've had our ups and downs, but I think with a little understanding on both sides, we should have a reasonably sound basis for a friendship.'

Brett did not speak for a considerable time, but by then his laughter had completely disappeared. 'I think you've summed up the situation with quite remarkable astuteness, not to mention imagination. You have been a little stupid, as you say yourself, but I'm duly grateful to you for your offer of friendship, and I accept happily. Only one thing puzzles me. Perhaps you could explain how you know so surely that I'm going to marry Lisa?'

Fern sat up, then stood up, and with fastidious care brushed the twigs and moss from her jeans. 'I can't tell you how I found out without incriminating someone else, but when I heard that Lisa was telling friends that, quote, "You and I only got engaged to please the old man" and that when he dies I'm leaving – or that's as near as I can remember.'

Fern straightened up and looked him straight in the eye, 'You gave me your word that you wouldn't tell anyone, so I

177

knew beyond any shadow of a doubt that you must have been serious if you'd broken your promise.'

Brett sighed, 'I don't suppose you'd believe me if I told you I had kept my word, and someone else must have given her the information?'

Fern threw out her hands. 'Who else knew, Brett? There was only you and me in the secret.'

'Yes, I guess that is the only conclusion you could come to. I'm more glad than ever that you'll continue our friendship, it's more than I deserve.'

He stood tall beside her. 'I think we'll head for home now. I've seen all I want to here. Thanks for speaking out so honestly, Fern.'

He walked to the horses and Fern followed him. The completely detached feeling had gone and in its place was only anguish, which told Fern how much she had hoped he would have denied the charge, even though she knew he couldn't because she had not told Lisa.

CHAPTER TEN

UNCLE HAMISH came home and the same day the barn was filled with hay, and the last bale of hay fitted into the lean-to by the cowshed.

It rained on Tuesday, huge heavy drops, slow at first, then building up to a crescendo of sound as the drops beat a continuous tattoo on the corrugated iron roof. The first day everybody received the rain with delight – 'This'll lay the dust', and 'We needed the rain to bring the paddocks away,' and 'Send her down, Hughie,' were commonly heard remarks. It rained that night, and it rained the next day, showing no sign of abating, if anything becoming heavier and shorter intervals between the storms. The heavy black clouds cut short the daylight and forced Kirsty to switch on the lights early in the evening.

Surface water lay in long strips across the paddocks, and soon concern was felt for the stopbank, built at great expense to protect this fertile valley.

Mr. Alexander, forced to stay inside, wandered from room to room looking out each window as if expecting to see some improvement. 'I was always pleased, Fern, that we bought our farm here away from the river. And yet one year it broke through and came roaring down the Valley sweeping fences and stock in front of it. That was before we all clubbed together and all the farmers were rated to pay for the Catchment Board improvements. Have you been down to the bridge?'

'Yes, it's running a banker. Rather scary really. The road is blocked in three places between here and Hokitika.'

That night the rain stopped, and they all breathed sighs of relief. The river dropped quickly, and the sun shone next day, but it was only a short reprieve. By lunchtime the clouds, dark and laden with rain, were overhead and the thunder rolled, and lightning lit the skies, then the heavens opened and made the previous storms seem like small showers.

About five the light was fading when Robbie knocked frantically on the door, then threw it open. He stood there, the water streaming off him. 'Quick! Get Brett! Hurry!'

Fern's feet took wings as she flew down the passage urged on by the urgency in Robbie's voice. 'Brett! Brett! Oh, good! Robbie wants you. He's at the back door. Quickly!'

Hamish and Kirsty were standing in the doorway when Brett got there.

'What's up, Robbie?'

'The O'Grady children, the two eldest, Troy and Karen, have been lost down the river. They left when the river was falling this morning, they were both on the same horse. They must have swum the horse to the Big Island, and then got caught in the storm. The horse turned up about an hour ago. They've just rung Ross, and he wants you and your jet-boat out on the river now. I'm to go with you. He's rung all the farmers on each side of the river to check their frontages in case the kids managed to get out of the river. He wants you, Fern, to go with him to the County huts where he'll set up the search and rescue headquarters, and Kirsty, Smithy will ring you about food.' He was shivering with the cold, but refused Kirsty's offer of tea, only waiting for Brett to finish struggling into his wet weather gear.

Mr. Alexander shut the door as they saw the lights from the ute light up the sky, as Brett swung round to hook up the trailer with the jet on. Seconds later they heard the roar of the ute's engine accelerating.

'Ross is head of the search and rescue team here. He'll want you as a nurse, so wrap up well and get over there,' Mr. Alexander advised.

Fern didn't want to leave Uncle Hamish – after all, he was her patient still, and the anxiety was bad for him. 'What about me? Are you going to sit there watching me when you could be of some help if they get those kids? I'm fine, and

180

Kirsty will be with me.'

Fern went to change into jeans and a thick jersey, and headed for the Smiths' house at the double, barely waiting to grab a parka from the washhouse.

Ross was still on the phone when she got there so she joined Smithy and Lisa in the kitchen. They were buttering sliced bread in stacks. 'Hi, Fern! No, don't strip off to help us, Ross will be through in a minute, and ready to leave. Lucky there are two huts by the bridge – the men will keep one for walkie-talkies, and schedules, etc. The women will use the other one for catering. See you down there in a couple of hours. You'll fancy a drop of tea by then.'

Fern followed Ross out when he finished on the phone. She didn't ask questions as they drove the comparatively short distance to the bridge. Ross talked enough for both of them. 'God save us. Why didn't they alert us at once? An hour of daylight is worth six in the dark. Poor little beggars out in this night. Half my team is cut off by the flooding – still, we've set everything in motion, now comes the hardest part, the waiting.'

Fern looked out the window as they crossed the bridge; the dull roar of the river was frightening, and Brett was out there in the rain and the dark, and Robbie too.

They pulled up by the hut and some men came out to carry the equipment into the hut. Ross went round giving quiet orders, answering a few questions, but there was not much talk; these men were practised and ready for any emergency.

'Can I do anything, Ross?' Fern asked.

'Not yet. Just sit over there in the corner out of the way. I'll call you if you're needed. The First Aid kit is on the table there. If the kids are found they could be suffering from exhaustion and exposure, depending on how long they've been in the water. Then on a night like this any of the searchers could get hurt, so I just want you ready. The doctor can't get through, nor can the police, who are normally part of this team.'

Fern knew she shouldn't, but could not help herself. 'What are their chances, Ross?'

Ross lit a cigarette. 'I wouldn't like to hazard a guess. Brett is our best hope. He was first on the river, and had a little daylight left. He'll search any islands that are out in the middle, and with luck he'll get them. Robbie will work the spotlight when it's dark. The kids, God help them, should be found tonight; if they aren't, it could take a week or so.'

One of the other men volunteered the information about other cases to prove Ross's point. To Fern it seemed callous, but her training told her different. These teams had to know and learn the statistics and experiences of other emergencies to know how best to find the missing or injured party.

Men came in from the rain and made their report, while Ross marked the large map he had spread out on the table, then sent them off to do another beat.

Someone else manned the phone, taking down reports from outlying farmers, these were written on a time sheet and the essence of the reports were written in the opposite column, and as soon as possible cleared with Ross on his map.

The only other man of the inside team was battling with a walkie-talkie which crackled and spat, the voices coming in horribly distorted.

Then Fern heard amongst the spluttering, 'Alexander has been in to get more fuel for the jet. Robbie reports no luck, and it's wild out there. Over.'

Ross turned to the operator. 'Tell him next time Brett comes in to send him up here to report I'm not having men's lives risked when there isn't much hope of finding them in the dark.'

Fern sat in her corner, listening, hoping one report would say the children were found, she knew their ages now, ten and twelve; Troy was the eldest.

Men still came and went, speaking quietly, and going out again, their faces grim but resolute. Later Smithy came in with tea and sandwiches. 'These are for the ones stuck in here, you other jokers come over to the hut and get yours. Send them in, Ross, as they report. They'll need something to keep them warm. No luck?'

'No luck,' Ross replied.

One man returned from the other hut. 'Smithy's got a huge fire going in there, a real little hell. That tea sure hit the right place. She's got that blonde there giving a hand, and Joe's wife and her sister Meg, and Maureen and Mrs. Johnstone. Where do you want me to go now? Oh, yes, the truck has come back with six spotlights and batteries.'

Ross nodded. 'Go and connect them up, ready, see they're all well labelled with the owner's name.'

There was a long period of quiet, but Fern found it impossible to relax, as did the others in the hut.

Then the phone rang, startling them all. Fern shut her eyes. Please let it be the kids safe. But it was another negative.

Brett came in about ten-thirty; he marked in his search area on the map.

Ross said, 'Call it off, Brett. You can't do much good till morning. I'll call the whole search off at eleven, and we'll start again at daybreak.'

Brett leaned over and pointed to a piece of land, which he said was cut off from the mainland by flood. 'I'd like to take a look there, Ross, then I'll sleep easy, knowing that if they went further than that they're gone anyway. I meant to look on the way back, but fuel was a problem. It would only take about a quarter of an hour straight down there and back. Robbie reckons he may have seen something. Have I your permission?'

Ross thought it over, and came to a decision. 'Okay. Just down, swing round it and come back. I don't have to tell you to watch for fences under the water there. Be back by eleven. Fern, take him over and get him a hot cup of tea. We don't need you here just now.'

Fern threw Ross a grateful glance and got a sly wink in return.

As they walked between the two huts, Fern found she had nothing to say. The sky lit up with a spectacular display of lightning, and the thunder shook the ground as if it was an earthquake.

'You're very wet,' Fern commented inanely. So much she wanted to say, but she couldn't.

Robbie was standing in front of the fire talking to Maureen, and sipping a cup of steaming hot tea. Other men in the room turned to look, and they found the answer as Brett shook his head.

Lisa suddenly saw Brett and rushed to meet him. Throwing her arms around him, taking no notice of his wet clothes, she hugged and kissed him. 'Oh, Brett baby, I've been so worried about you!'

Brett put her aside gently and took his tea. 'Thanks, Smithy. Hell of a night out there.'

'Are you and Robbie finished now?' Smithy asked casually.

'No. One more short trip, and then we'll call it off. We'll be back by eleven. Ross says he's going to pack it in then.'

'No, Brett, no. You've done your turn. Let someone else go. Ross has no right to send you out again. I'll tell him so.'

Brett caught her as she went to do that. 'You don't understand, Lisa, I asked Ross to let us go. Ready, Robbie?'

Fern saw Maureen and Robbie holding hands, but not speaking. And as Robbie nodded to Brett, Fern realized that at a time like this there were no words appropriate.

Brett put his drained cup on the bench. 'That was great, Smithy.' Lisa was still clinging to his arm as if she wouldn't let him go.

He took Fern's hand with his free one. 'Take Lisa home soon, Fern. This is no place for her.' He squeezed her hand. 'Wish you were wearing your dark glasses.'

'Oh, Brett, so do I!' She saw his blue eyes gleam.

'Never mind, Fern, there'll be another day tomorrow.'

Fern carried a tray of tea back to Ross and his men. 'Brett

asked me to take Lisa home, she's crying over in the other hut.'

'Stupid twit!' Ross couldn't hide his anger. 'Yeah, you take her home. I don't think we'll be needing you, but I'll ring if I do. Take Brett's Holden, I'll go home with Mum.'

As Fern went to leave, the phone rang stridently. As the man answered it, Fern waited.

'They've got them! Oh, lord, they've got them! They're safe!' He put the phone down and sat in the corner where Fern had spent most of the night. The tears ran down his face, then a couple of men stood in front of him, while Ross took the phone. 'Right, great, great. You'll keep them till the morning. A lot of us will sleep well tonight. Sure they're okay? Yes? Tell them they're a pair of flaming beauts. Hooroo!'

'That's it, Jim. Start calling them in, and check them off. But first get on to the post by the river and try to stop Brett.'

Fern just stood. It was fantastic news. She knew that most of the searchers had felt it was hopeless.

Ross said, 'Well, that's it. The kids got swept off their horse at the bottom of Big Island, but they hung together, and Troy managed to catch some willows on the next lot, and they stayed there for an hour yelling their heads off. Poor brats, even saw their parents on the bank, but were up to their waists in the water by then, and their voices were drowned in the flood.

'Then a huge matai tree stranded on the island beside them and they took a chance. Nervy little jokers! They rode it perhaps a mile before getting off, luckily close to Linn's farm.'

The man in the corner stood up with a smile, ear to ear. 'I'd like to thank you all . . . I'll get home to my wife. Okay, Ross?'

As he went out, everyone either shook his hand or whacked him on the back.

Ross, seeing Fern's puzzled look, said, 'That was

O'Grady, father of the kids.'

Fern looked at Mr. O'Grady. She'd sat there all night, not knowing what private hell he was going through as he answered each phone call, and heard negative each time, noting it in the right column, with careful precision.

'Okay, scram, Fern. Pick up Lisa. We'll hang on here till all the men are in. By the time you get home we'll be close on your heels. We'll leave the dishes in the sink tonight. We'll come and clean up in the morning.'

Fern, although disappointed that they hadn't been able to stop Brett, was sure he'd be home soon. After all, he'd come back twice now.

She got Lisa and had a few words with Smithy, then drove home. She let Lisa out at Smith's. 'Leave the kids where they are tonight, Lisa. No use taking them out in the rain again. I'd get to bed if I were you.'

Fern garaged the Holden and ran for the house. Kirsty was still up, so was first to hear the good news.

'You get off to bed, Kirsty. I'll sit up and wait for Brett. I'll pop in and see Uncle Hamish, and see how Sally and Simon are.'

She told him about the children, gave him his pill for the night. 'You didn't need me. You're really looking better. 'Night. I'll switch the light off.'

Sally lay neat and straight in her bed, while 'Me Jack' had rolled himself into a ball, with most of the blankets on the floor. Fern straightened the bed and kissed each child, then left the room on tiptoe.

'There now, Fern. I'm thinking Brett will want a complete change, so I've put them on the cylinder to warm. Wonderful to think of those brave youngsters surviving in that flood. It seems a miracle. I'm away to my bed – you'll see to Brett?'

Fern just sat feeling the wonderful happiness of having been part of an organization that had found the children she'd never even seen, but felt she knew so well.

She made herself coffee, thinking it was an hour since

she'd left the huts. It was time the rest got home. Then she saw the lights of a car flash on the window as it turned in the drive. She sat waiting. The car stopped at the back steps and she sat still, waiting for Brett to come through the door, her heart filled with a wild elation.

There was a knock, and Smithy and Ross came in. Fern felt frozen. 'Sorry about this, Fern – Brett and Robbie didn't come back. I'm not much at breaking news gently. Some searchers saw the jet hit a log that was floating well down in the water, and they said it was splintered to bits. We'll get the search under way at daybreak. I've rung all the chaps, there'll be a full turn-out.'

Smithy put her arm around Fern. 'Would you like me to stay here with you tonight? Ross reckoned it better not to tell Kirsty or Hamish. Let them get a good night's sleep, and maybe by the time they wake, they'll be found.'

Fern shook her head. 'I'll be fine. They say miracles don't happen twice – those small kids got out, didn't they? But Brett and Robbie, they'll make it too.'

'Have an aspirin or something, Fern. You've got to be on deck tomorrow, whatever the news. We'll cut along home now, Mum and me. It's rotten luck, but I knew we could count on you to take it sensibly. We're not going to tell Lisa, there's no point in having her screaming around the house all night. Good night, Fern, try and get a bit of rest.' He patted her shoulder and went out.

'Call us if you want anything, Fern. Just walk right into our bedroom. You'll take this hard, I know. But think of O'Grady – we'll be feeling like him tomorrow morning.'

She left the kitchen with a heavy tread which told its own story; she was usually so quick and light on her feet.

Fern got up and switched the lights off. No use having Kirsty wake, and seeing the lights on come to see what was the matter.

The rain eased off and finally stopped.

Fern sat at the table her head in her hands, waiting for the dawn. She had another cup of coffee about three, then about an hour later she heard the first bird call. Looking up, she saw the clouds had cleared away, and the sun was tipping the small scudding clouds a delicate pink.

She stretched her cramped bones and stood up. The first bird was still trilling its song, then another joined it, and another, until the whole plantation seemed alive with music. This must be the dawn chorus. She went out to the seat she had shared with Brett on Christmas night.

The first bird was still louder than the rest. He must be the waker-upper. Fern smiled; the other birds were probably fed up to the back teeth at being woken by his tune every morning! She imagined the two that flew to the plum tree, saying 'You can go off some people!' like Robbie was always saying. What a stupid thing to think of!

She watched the sun herald his arrival, with a fantastic display of colours shaping and changing the sky. Then one little tip was seen over Mount Graham.

She didn't think of Brett and Robbie as alive, she didn't think of them as dead, she kept steadily in front of her Brett saying, 'Never mind, Fern, there'll be another day tomorrow.' This was Brett's new day, so she would wait for him.

Ross joined her about five. 'You been up all night, kid? I've just had a ring from down river. Brett and Robbie walked into Tim's house a while ago. They're on their way home now, could be here any minute. Tim said his phone was out of order so he had to go across the road to ring up.'

Fern stood up, and put out her hand to touch Ross, then crumpled at his feet, just as a strange car swept up the drive and braked beside them.

She heard Ross say, 'She fainted. She sat up all night waiting and then when I told her you were both okay, she flaked out.'

Fern knew he was being quite ridiculous, she had never fainted in her whole life.

'Sorry about this, Fern. I'm all wet, but I'm going to

carry you inside.'

Fern relaxed; that was Brett, he knew she wouldn't faint. Inside he put her down on the Colonial couch. 'I'll get you a drink, Fern.'

She sat up and swallowed obediently. 'Lie down, I'll be back in a jiffy. I've got to get into dry clothes.'

'They're in the cylinder warming. Kirsty put them there last night.'

Then Fern started to cry quietly, and could not stop. It seemed so long ago that Kirsty was standing there telling her to see to Brett.

Brett came back and lifted her on to his knee while he mopped up her tears. 'I thought you'd forgotten how to cry, Fern, when you stopped loving me.'

'I did not, too – stop loving you, I mean.'

'Good, because you're going to marry me, Fern, my darling.'

Fern sniffed rudely. 'There you go again! You don't even propose properly, you just order me to accept you.'

'And are you going to accept me?'

'You bet your sweet life I am! I was going to be big-hearted and generous and let Lisa have you, but after what I went through last night, I'm going to stay here and look after you. Poor Lisa!'

'Poor Lisa, nothing,' Brett said firmly. 'You've got it all wrong about her. She's going to marry a chap in Christ-church, her boss, by the way – seems to be becoming a habit with her.'

Suddenly it struck them both as hilariously funny, and they laughed madly together.

'I won't make you a good wife, Brett. I don't know enough about cars and boats' insides, and I don't know any-thing about breeding cows and horses and dogs.'

Brett kissed her on the cheek. 'Serious deficiencies, my pet. However, I'll overlook them if you'll promise to love, honour, and obey me.'

'You'd better leave out the last one. I'll never become a

"Whatever you say, darling" wife. I'll fight with you.'

Brett smiled, 'Don't I know it! But think of the fun we'll have making it up.'

Fern eyed him solemnly. 'I like you, Brett Alexander.'

'And I like you too, Fern Fraser, even if you are a little stupid sometimes, and are so quick to jump to the wrong conclusion. For instance, I didn't tell Lisa about our engagement. She just kept asking Smithy and Ross questions, and then made a lucky stab. And do you know who the real Jack of "Me Jack" is? None other than Lisa's intended, and he dotes on the kids. She came over here for what you might call sentimental reasons, and when she found out she couldn't get me on my knees, then she decided to have a go to see how much trouble she could stir up. She's a cunning minx, she knew all the time Smithy was lying in the bedroom, that's why she made up all that guff. She'll be leaving as soon as the floods go down.'

Fern gasped, 'But all that concern over you last night at the hut . . .'

Brett laughed. 'Lisa always had a fine turn for the dramatic. She grabbed her chance, and played it to the full. And you, like a ninny, believe her. Really, you're not very bright.'

Fern tried to struggle off his knee, but he held her easily. 'Don't try so hard to get away, or I might let you go. After all, it's not every bloke who'll marry a stupid girl.'

Fern swung round.

'That's my girl!' He kissed her, and she knew that she would never leave the Matai Valley. The hills were really the Hills of Home.

Golden Harlequin Library

A Treasury of Harlequin Romances!

Many of the all time favorite Harlequin Romance Novels have not been available, until now, since the original printing. But on this special introductory offer, they are yours in an exquisitely bound, rich gold hardcover with royal blue imprint. Three complete unabridged novels in each volume. And the cost is so very low you'll be amazed!

Handsome, Hardcover Library Editions at Paperback Prices! ONLY $1.95 each volume.

This very special collection of classic Harlequin Romances would be a distinctive addition to your library. And imagine what a delightful gift they'd make for any Harlequin reader!

Start your collection now. See reverse of this page for **SPECIAL INTRODUCTORY OFFER!**

v